THE CLUE OF THE
BROKEN BLADE

"THAT LOOKS LIKE STEALING!"

The Clue of the Broken Blade   *Frontispiece (Page 158)*

THE CLUE OF THE
BROKEN BLADE

By
FRANKLIN W. DIXON

ILLUSTRATED BY
PAUL LAUNE

NEW YORK
GROSSET & DUNLAP
PUBLISHERS

CONTENTS

vi Contents

CHAPTER I

THE MYSTERIOUS TRUCK

"OUCH! Have a heart!"

With a snort Joe Hardy tumbled to the floor while his brother Frank stood over him, waving a folded umbrella.

"Give up?" grinned Frank, poking at Joe's ribs.

There was a moment of silence.

"No!" came the sudden answer.

With a bound the younger boy was back on his feet brandishing a second umbrella. For a moment the fight was nip and tuck. Suddenly Joe's weapon found its mark. Down went Frank.

"Boys! Boys! What is going on here? Stop it this minute!"

Her face white with alarm, Aunt Gertrude stood peering over her glasses into the disordered living room. Frank pulled himself upright, rubbing his side. "Don't worry, Aunt

Gertrude, we're just practicing," he reassured her.

"Practicing?" snorted the boys' elderly relative. "Practicing how to kill yourselves. Gracious! Just look at this room. Chairs turned over, your mother's clean rugs all mussed——"

Joe went over and patted his father's sister on her shoulder. "There, there, Aunt Gertrude, we'll fix everything up again. We were just learning how to duel. You see, we're going to be in a play and have to know the way to do it."

"Yes, Chet Morton and his sister Iola want us to take part in a mystery play being put on for charity," Frank explained further, while Aunt Gertrude looked at them skeptically.

"Hmph. A play, indeed," she said indignantly. "What sort of play is it where two boys have to stick umbrellas into each other——"

"Oh, we're going to use real swords in the play, Auntie," Joe interrupted mischievously. "Sharp ones, too. Golly, we'll——"

"That will be quite enough," snapped the woman. "I'll have to speak to your father about it when he comes in. I'm sure he would not approve of his sons taking part in any dangerous duels."

With a defiant shake of her head Aunt Gertrude flounced off, leaving the brothers convulsed with mirth.

"I'm afraid she isn't going to help our acting career very much," Joe observed dryly.

"No, she'll probably be telling Dad about it any minute. I think I hear him coming now."

Heavy footfalls sounded on the veranda. The door opened to admit a tall, handsome man with graying hair and keen blue eyes. He gave a start as he surveyed the scene in the living room.

"Hmm. Has there been an earthquake?" he queried.

"Hello, Dad!" both boys exclaimed in the same breath.

An instant later they were exchanging sheepish grins and eyeing their parent uncertainly.

"We were just dueling, Dad," Frank offered finally. "Aunt Gertrude——"

"Yes, with your mother away I can imagine what Aunt Gertrude thinks of you," Mr. Hardy winked, waving a hand toward an overturned chair. "Well, come into the study, both of you. I have some interesting things to tell you."

The brothers needed no second invitation, for such a bidding from their father, the famous detective, usually meant that adventure was in the offing. Fenton Hardy laid a bulging brief case on his desk and sank into his swivel chair.

"Hard assignment," he said, motioning toward the portfolio. "I think I have three of the criminals rounded up, but a fourth has eluded me thus far." He paused and looked out the window thoughtfully. "But that's not what I especially want to speak to you boys about."

Frank and Joe sat on the edge of their chairs, their eyes eager with anticipation. Mr. Hardy spoke.

"I have reason to believe that one of the biggest groups in crime is operating under our very noses," he burst forth.

"You mean right here in Bayport, Dad?" Joe exclaimed.

Mr. Hardy shook his head. "I'm not certain they've reached Bayport yet, but they're in our vicinity, possibly as near as Aberdeen."

Frank looked at his brother. "Whew! That really sounds like something. What are they up to, anyhow?"

"Stealing is their principal occupation," replied the detective grimly, "but they won't stop short of killing people who get in their way. Their scheme, boys, is about as clever and brazen a one as I've ever heard."

Frank and Joe squirmed expectantly as their father paused.

"It seems that the ringleaders own a fleet of motor trucks. Their plan is to have their drivers take these huge vehicles to wharves or railroad depots, and——"

"And steal merchandise being unloaded from ships and trains, I'll bet. Is that right, Dad?" Joe asked impatiently.

Mr. Hardy could barely conceal a smile. "Your statement happens to hit the nail right on the head, son. That's just what they're doing. The result is that thousands of dollars' worth of valuable goods are disappearing every week.''

Frank studied his father's face hopefully. "Are you going to let us help you on the case, Dad?''

His parent nodded. "I was coming to that, Frank. From the way things look I shall be busy for some time on a certain angle of the case. Meanwhile I wonder whether you boys might like to follow one clue I have——''

"Will we! I'll say so," the younger lad exclaimed. "Dad, you know we'll do anything we can to help you.''

Fenton Hardy looked at his sons gravely. "Boys, I'm afraid these men we are after are extremely vicious. They'll stop at nothing if they suspect you're trailing them. Don't take any unnecessary risks.''

"We'll be careful," Frank promised.

"Very well. The freighter *Nordic* is due to dock in the Aberdeen harbor tonight with a load of silver pieces for the Liberty Company. Some of these are very old and extremely valuable. I have reason to believe that the trucking thieves may attempt to steal this cargo. Your job will be to check up, see what happens, and then report to me.''

Eagerly the brothers rushed upstairs to pack. They decided to put on old overalls as a disguise but carry good clothes with them. After a parting word with their father they jumped into Frank's car and headed for the broad highway.

"We ought to make it in an hour easily," Joe observed as they hummed along. "Look, there's the Old Mill Restaurant already. How about a bite of supper?"

Twenty minutes later they were off again. Just as dusk was falling they entered the outskirts of the bay city of Aberdeen.

"I hope we're not too late to catch the ship, Frank."

"We made good time and couldn't have reached here any sooner, Joe. Look, isn't that the harbor?"

Frank nosed the car through a narrow, crowded street. Presently they found themselves at a huge wharf.

"There's the *Nordic*," Joe whispered tensely. "It's just coming in. Boy, what luck!"

A large cargo vessel was being warped into her berth by two snorting tugs. Their hearts pounding in suppressed excitement, the two Hardy boys made their way through the crowd of idle onlookers, reaching the edge of the dock just as the ship came alongside.

"If any of the band Dad mentioned are planning to steal the *Nordic's* freight, they should be arriving soon," Frank breathed.

There was a loud clank of chains and a strain of hawsers as the vessel was made fast. Directly opposite where the boys were standing, a large door swung open in the ship's side.

"The cargo hold, Frank! Boy, isn't she loaded! Wonder if——"

Frank clutched his brother's arm. Amid a deafening roar a huge covered truck lumbered up, stopping beside them.

"Maybe that driver is one of the thieves," the boy said tensely.

"We'll watch the fellow," replied his brother.

"Where's the supercargo o' this ship?" demanded the driver, peering down at the boys. "I'm in a hurry. Got to haul away some valuable boxes without delay. The company don't want 'em stolen."

The brothers gazed at a name painted on the side of the truck. Liberty Company!

"We'll try to find him for you," offered Frank. As the brothers moved off, he whispered to Joe, "Guess we're on the wrong track. But we'll watch and be sure that the fellow doesn't pull any funny business."

"Right," agreed Joe, approaching a ship's officer who had just stepped off the gangplank and was carrying a sheaf of papers in his hand.

"Have you some boxes for the Liberty Company?" asked Frank.

By this time the truckman had approached and presented his credentials. Everything seemed to be in order, so the driver was given permission to load the boxes.

"You guys want to earn some money?" he asked, turning to the Hardys. "I want to get this stuff on as soon as possible."

"Sure," said Frank. Then as the man went to unlock the back of the van, he whispered, "Even if we haven't caught any thieves, at least we can help this driver get away before any of the gang arrive."

"Think I'll look over all the trucks here," suggested Joe. "Be back in a minute."

He found nothing suspicious, so returned to assist with the loading. In twenty minutes the task was accomplished, the Hardys paid, and the driver was off.

"Our first assignment turned out to be a wild goose chase," sighed Frank, as the two boys walked to their car.

"I'm afraid Dad will be disappointed," added his brother.

They had gone barely half a mile along the highway out of Aberdeen when a pair of dazzling headlights bore down on them.

"Why doesn't that fellow watch where he's going?" Frank exploded, veering toward one side.

There was a roar as the glare came closer. The boy began to toot his horn. He and his brother held their breaths.

"He's going to hit us, Frank!" Joe shouted.

Just as a crash seemed imminent there was a screech of brakes. A large truck slithered to a stop not three feet from their car.

"Frank! Look at the sign! It says 'Liberty Company'!" Joe exclaimed excitedly.

The driver leaned out of his cab. "Sorry to scare you," he yelled. "I'm in a hurry. Got to meet a ship."

Frank eyed his brother significantly, then jumped from their car. He rushed over to the big vehicle, with Joe on his heels.

"Did you say you were to meet a ship?" the elder lad inquired. "Was it by any chance the *Nordic*?"

"That's it, boys. Say, tell me, is she in yet?" He seemed to be looking at them anxiously.

"She's in, all right," returned Frank. "We just came from there, and helped to load one of your company's trucks."

"What!" The man stared at them aghast. "Do you mean you helped load a Liberty Company truck?"

Frank nodded, his heart skipping a beat. The driver leaped out, his face distorted with rage and dismay.

"Boys, there's only one Liberty Company truck that's supposed to meet the *Nordic,* and this is it!" he groaned.

CHAPTER II

A CLUE

THE truck driver showed his credentials to the boys. They included a letter of praise from the president of the company for long and efficient service. Sick at heart over their terrible mistake, the Hardys finally related the whole story to the man.

"Well, it ain't as if you helped that thief on purpose," said their listener. "Naturally you didn't know what the fellow was up to."

"Just the same we should have been more cautious," Frank mourned. "After all, we're supposed to be detectives. *Some* detectives we are!"

The man blinked at them. "Detectives! You boys detectives!" he cried.

Frank introduced himself and Joe. The man smiled broadly and held out a huge hand. "Put 'er there, boys. I'm mighty glad to know you," he said heartily. "I've heard tell of your dad. I'm Tom Klip, best driver the Liberty Company—" He suddenly checked himself. "Guess I ain't the best driver any longer," he went on sorrowfully. "I'll get fired for losin' those boxes, sure as shootin'. It's really all my fault, bein' late gettin' to the ship."

Frank knit his brow. "I'm wondering where

that other driver got his credentials. Some printing plant must have done a good job of making out false bills of lading.''

''You're right, Frank,'' his brother agreed. ''Golly, if we could find the printer we'd have an important clue.''

The older boy nodded. ''Yes, and here's an idea, too.''

For several moments Frank whispered with the others in the darkness. This was not the first time the Hardy brothers had found themselves swiftly laying plans for the solution of some desperate crime.

As true sons of their famous father, one of the greatest detectives the country had ever known, Frank and Joe were rapidly achieving reputations of their own. The first of their adventures was told in ''The Tower Treasure,'' wherein the boys helped their father find some stolen loot after a baffling search.

Their mother, Laura Mildred Hardy, and their Aunt Gertrude sometimes looked askance at the interest the boys took in detective work, though inwardly they were proud of their youthful ability. Fenton Hardy, on the other hand, was openly delighted that his sons were following in his footsteps.

As in the present instance, Mr. Hardy many times had actually turned over the task of solving a mystery to his sons when he himself was occupied with some other case. Though the solution of these riddles often led to great danger, Frank and Joe never once had flinched in their attempts to clear them up. This had been shown in their latest adventure, which was a hunt for spies, in a story called "The Mystery of the Flying Express."

As they now stood on the lonely road near Aberdeen, both brothers felt that they were about to embark on one of the most exciting cases of their young careers.

"I'm afraid it's too late to do anything about the robbery, fellows," Tom Klip was saying with a pessimistic shake of his head. "You'll never be able to catch that other truck driver now. He's plumb gone."

"He certainly will be gone if we don't get started after him right away," Frank said decisively. "Tom, suppose you go back to your company's headquarters and stay near a phone. We'll get in touch with you as soon as we find a clue."

"Well, all right, if you say so, but——"

Before the truckman could finish, Frank and Joe had jumped into their car and turned it around. With a toot of their horn they sped back toward Aberdeen.

"I've a hunch where we can pick up a clue," the older boy said between set teeth. "We'll ask the gatekeeper at that railroad crossing near the wharf."

Joe looked thoughtful. "The joke will be on us if Tom Klip is the gangsters' driver and the other fellow turns out to be honest."

"His papers looked authentic," said Frank. "Anyhow, we'll find out for certain if we can catch the other fellow. Here we are."

Frank put on the brakes as they approached the lights of a grade crossing. "I hope the gate-tender is still on duty—yes, there he is, Joe."

Stopping the car, he jumped out with his brother right behind him. A grizzled old man standing by the track watched them curiously.

"A truck? Sure, there's been plenty o' trucks passin' here this evenin'," he cackled in response to their questions.

"But the one we're looking for has Liberty Company painted on the sides," Frank pressed.

The old man tapped his pipe. "Liberty Company? Hm. There was a Liberty Company truck. Let's see, about half an hour ago, near as I can recollect. Crossed both ways."

"That's the one," Joe exclaimed, trying not to show his excitement. "Which way did it go?"

"Well, let's see. I cain't remember for sartin', but I kind o' think he took that there left-hand fork. That road goes off to the mountains. Mind you, now, I cain't be sure——"

With a hasty word of thanks the boys hopped into the front seat and drove off in the direction the man had indicated. As the lights of Aberdeen were left behind, Joe's doubts began to mount.

"How are we ever going to find one solitary truck 'way out here in all this blackness?" he speculated dismally. "Look, there isn't even a house or a gasoline station where we could make any inquiries."

"There's no harm in our trying," replied his brother, though he too began to have misgivings. "One thing's sure. That heavy truck can't go as fast as we can."

"No, but it has a good head start. Say, what's up there? Looks as if we're going into some pretty deep woods," Joe exclaimed.

The road was becoming narrower. A few moments later the brothers found themselves hemmed in by giant trees which swayed weirdly in the wind.

"Golly, what a dismal place," Joe remarked. Suddenly he seized his brother's sleeve, saying, "Frank! Isn't that a light up ahead?"

Instantly Frank jammed on the brakes and switched off both engine and head lamps. For several moments the boys strained their eyes and ears.

"Are you sure you saw a light, Joe?"

"I thought I did. About a hundred yards ahead. There it is again."

There was no mistaking the eerie glow filtering through the trees not far distant. As they watched, it vanished. A few seconds later it appeared again.

"Come on, Joe, we'll investigate," Frank whispered tensely.

Their hearts pounding, they left the car and stealthily advanced along the road. Gradually the light grew brighter. It seemed to glow from the deep woods some distance from the edge of the road. Frank in the lead halted and raised a finger to his lips.

"Sh!" he warned. "Let's strike through the woods, Joe. The wind's making enough noise to drown out sounds we make, but we'd better be careful anyhow."

Their first steps through the underbrush brought forth the loud snap of dry twigs; otherwise, there was no sound but the brushing of branch against branch.

"Guess we're all right so far," Frank breathed. "Come on."

Gingerly they advanced, trying desperately to avoid stepping on twigs and branches in their path. The strange light wavered mysteriously somewhere ahead of them. Once it almost caught them directly in its rays.

"We'd better crawl from here on," Frank whispered finally, dropping to the ground.

For some time they struggled through the dense thicket. Suddenly Frank whispered excitedly:

"Look, Joe! There's the man we're after!"

"He's painting out the Liberty Company lettering on the truck!" said his brother in a muffled tone.

Quivering with excitement, the boys watched the strange scene. Within a small clearing not fifty feet away the man could be seen standing on a ladder braced against the side of the van.

In one hand he held a powerful flashlight; in the other, a paint brush. Now and then he would pause to play the beam over the work he was doing.

"He has just about finished," Joe murmured. "No, he's going after that other bucket of paint. What's he up to now?"

"We'll soon find out. Oh, he's moving his ladder to a new place. Look, it's red paint he's using this time. He's putting on another sign!"

Now and then above the sighing of the wind the lads could hear the deep grunts of satisfaction as the man worked. The flashlight rays played about eerily as he swayed slightly at his task.

"There goes a 'J,'" Joe whispered. "Now an 'O,' 'L,'—'Jolson,' it says."

"Here comes another word. 'R,' 'A'——"

"'Radio,'" finished Joe. "Is that all? No! There's the last word. 'Shop.' 'Jolson Radio Shop.'"

"Boy, if this isn't tracking down a thief I don't know what is!" Frank exulted under his breath. "Still, we have to——"

"Look, he must be tired, Frank. He's lying down on the ground. Wonder if he'll go to sleep."

The boys watched tensely. The man had rolled up his coat to form a pillow and had stretched himself on the ground. Suddenly, to their dismay, the beam of his flashlight went out abruptly, plunging the place in darkness.

"What shall we do, Frank?" Joe whispered.

"We must take that truck!"

"The driver may wake up."

"We'll have to take that chance. Let's see how he came in here from the road. Did you bring your light?"

"Here it is. We'd better hold off a while. He may not be asleep yet."

After a little wait they could hear the tell-tale sounds of snoring coming through the deep gloom. Stealthily they crept into the clearing.

"Stand in front of the truck and snap on the flashlight ahead," said Frank under his breath. "Then the rays won't get in his eyes and wake him up."

The beam cut a swath of brilliance through the blackness. Instantly Joe snapped the light off again. Frank, who had been standing guard over the sleeping driver, joined him. "The truck is parked ready to start right off. There's a steep slope going down to the main road right in front of it," Joe informed his brother.

"Good! That means we can let it roll before we start the engine. We ought to get away before that driver can wake up and intercept us."

"Are we ready?"

Together the boys listened with bated breaths. Monotonously the man's snoring continued. Frank touched his brother's sleeve.

"All ready, Joe!" he said almost soundlessly.

CHAPTER III

THERE was a faint squeak as Frank stepped onto the running board of the big truck. The driver, snoring on the ground near-by, made no movement.

"Go ahead!" whispered Joe, gently nudging his brother. "The fellow's still asleep."

Gingerly the older boy crawled behind the wheel. As Joe walked ahead, playing his flashlight and motioning to his brother to proceed, Frank released the brake. The big truck began to roll. Down the crude wagon track Frank guided it for about two hundred feet. Then Joe hopped inside, the headlights were turned on, and the speed was increased.

"What's that noise, Frank?" Joe asked his brother in sudden consternation.

From somewhere through the trees ahead of them a loud rumble was growing rapidly in intensity.

"It's a train. The railroad tracks must be near here. That's great! The noise will drown out the sound of our motor."

As the rumble increased to a roar, Frank threw on the power. By the time the raucous clatter of the passing train subsided the Hardys were swinging into the main road.

"Whew," whistled Joe, "between the train and us there was enough racket to wake up any sleeper. Wonder if the fellow has missed the truck yet."

Presently Frank slowed his speed. "Here's the road we took. Our car isn't far away. Why don't you get it, find a policeman, and see if you can catch that driver? I'll take this load to the Liberty Company in Aberdeen."

"Good enough. I'll meet you there as soon as I can. So long!"

With a wave of his hand Joe leaped to the ground and was off to the Hardy car. At top speed he headed for Aberdeen.

"Pardon me, sir, but can you direct me to the police station?" he asked a bystander as he entered the town.

"Third block on your right," came the answer.

Two minutes later he marched up the steps and confronted a sleepy desk sergeant.

"What's that, young man? You say you've located a criminal? Williams!" he called. A patrolman emerged from an adjoining room. "Go along with this young fellow and check up on his yarn," snapped the sergeant. "Sounds like a fairy story to me."

The officer followed Joe to the latter's car and the two sped off. The Hardy lad related the high points of the experience of his brother and himself.

"If he's still asleep we won't have any trouble capturing him," the lad finished.

"And if he woke up and left, who's going to prove this isn't a lot of nonsense?" demanded the policeman.

Joe slowed the car as they approached the spot where he and Frank had parked previously. "I think we'd better walk the rest of the way, Officer. He'll hear us coming otherwise," suggested Joe.

"All right, young man, lead the way. But it'll go hard with you if this is a practical joke."

The Hardy boy began to have misgivings. Suppose the truck driver had awakened long before this and vanished? Nevertheless, Joe crawled on through a short cut with Officer Williams following.

Suddenly Joe stopped. "I think I can make out the clearing up there ahead," he whispered.

They listened. There was no sound. "If he's sleeping he certainly isn't snoring," Williams muttered dryly. "Better snap on your light and we'll have a look."

Joe's heart skipped a beat. He drew out his flashlight and pressed the button, almost giving vent to a whoop of delight as a prone figure loomed up in the rays.

"That's the fellow, Officer! That's the truck driver!" he cried.

With a bound Williams reached the clearing.

"Hey, you! Wake up!" he called, leaning down and shaking the figure roughly.

"W-w-what the—say, what's goin' on here?" growled a sleepy voice.

The figure suddenly sat bolt upright. Seeing Joe, the man scowled blackly.

"Oh, so it's you!" he hissed.

"This is the man whose truck my brother and I helped to load," Joe declared.

"What's your name?" demanded Williams, frowning at the man.

"Moe Gordon. I ain't done nothin' wrong, Chief, honest! Nobody can prove nothin' against me."

"Where's your truck?" snapped the officer.

"The truck? Right over the . . . say, where is it? You stole it!" he shouted, pointing a finger at Joe. "That young upstart stole it, Chief!"

"Save all that for the judge," ordered the officer. "Come on, get up. You're going along with us."

Cringing and muttering under his breath, the culprit walked between Joe and Officer Williams. "You'll pay for this *plenty*," he snarled at the Hardy lad.

"Keep your mouth shut," snapped Williams, pushing the man into the car. Turning to Joe, he said, "All right, young fellow, take us back to the police station."

Having deposited Gordon and the policeman safely at headquarters, Joe turned the car about and headed for the Liberty Company. He inquired the way at a gas station and was directed to a large group of buildings about half a mile ahead.

"That you, Joe?" a familiar figure greeted him.

Frank stood in a lighted doorway as his brother drove into the factory yard.

"Hello," said Joe. "I've brought good news!"

"Did you capture him?"

"Certainly did, with the help of Officer Williams of the Aberdeen Police!"

"What's all the rumpus about?" drawled a third voice just then. "Well, if it isn't Frank's brother!" Tom Klip cried, stepping forward and shaking hands with Joe. "So you caught that crook, did you, Joe? By jiminy, you two fellers have certainly done me a big favor. Saved my job and saved the company a lot of money."

"Before we lose any more time, let's unload the truck," Frank suggested. "First thing we know, somebody else will steal those boxes."

The three went to the rear of one of the buildings where Frank had parked the truck.

"The stuff goes in the warehouse here," said Tom. "Won't take us long to get it inside. After that how about you boys coming home with me for a few winks of sleep?"

Rest would be welcome indeed after the excitement of the evening. The brothers worked hurriedly under the man's direction, and in no time the valuable goods were stacked safely in the warehouse.

"Thanks, boys. Now for home. Joe, how about tellin' us what happened and how you caught that crook," suggested Tom Klip.

As they drove to a near-by residential section the Hardy lad related his adventure.

"Of course, we'll have to prove to the police that we're really on the level," he concluded. "I promised them we'd come back at eight o'clock in the morning."

Tom Klip made the boys comfortable for the rest of the night. It seemed to the Hardys that they had just touched their pillows when their host aroused them, saying it was time to keep their appointment at police headquarters.

"Gosh, I hate to move," groaned Joe. "What a dark, dreary day!"

At that moment a car stopped outside. An officer came to the Klip door. Joe and Frank hurried downstairs to speak to the fellow.

"We're looking for a Mister Klip so we can find the Hardy brothers," said an authoritative voice.

"We're the ones you're seeking," replied Frank.

"The Chief wants you at headquarters, boys," said the uniformed man. "Better make it snappy. Follow me."

The Hardys entered their parked car.

"I wonder what all the hurry's about?" speculated Joe. "I'm hungry."

"We'll soon find out," said Frank. "My, that fellow certainly isn't wasting any time. Hope we don't blow a tire going around corners——"

The police car ahead suddenly slithered to a stop. Its occupants jumped out and ran over to the two in the other machine.

"Just had a radio report that there's a bad fire at headquarters, fellows. Follow me if you can, but I've got to make it fast," called the officer.

Frank put on speed and they tore after the police car, whose siren now was screaming.

"I smell smoke," Joe exclaimed. "Look, there's the blaze. We're almost there."

As he turned the next corner, Frank had to jam on the brakes to avoid crashing into a parked fire engine. The street was full of shouting firemen and squirming lengths of hose. Over the scene there hung a pall of smoke, with billows of solid flame spurting from the burning building.

"Boy, that's a real fire," Joe murmured, quivering with excitement. "Maybe we'd better give the firemen a hand. They need it."

The lads raced to a group of fire fighters and seized a heavy length of hose.

"Help 'em carry it over yonder," thundered the fire chief, panting heavily.

Together the boys struggled with the heavy tubing, getting nearer the flames inch by inch. Suddenly Joe gave a cry.

"Frank! There he goes!"

"Who?"

"Gordon! The truck driver we caught! Quick! After him!"

A racing figure, fitfully illuminated by the light of the fire, whisked past them. Like a shot Joe followed. Down the cluttered street he tore, with Frank some distance behind. Just then the older lad caught the glitter of light on metal. Then came a loud *clang* which sent a chill to his heart. A second fire engine was just turning the corner into their street.

"Look out, Joe! You'll be run down!" he yelled, his lungs almost bursting.

The boy, oblivious of all but the fleeing Gordon, was running headlong toward the corner.

"Joe! Look out!" called Frank.

There was a fierce screeching of brakes as the giant fire apparatus veered crazily into the gutter. Frank's heart sank as a cry sounded through the pall of smoke.

CHAPTER IV

MOE GORDON DISAPPEARS

"Wow! That was too close for comfort!"

The big fire truck had just crashed past, missing Joe Hardy by inches. The boy watched it career toward the curbing, then straighten again. Frank was glad to see his brother out of danger.

"Now, where's Gordon? Gee, I've lost him," sighed the younger brother.

The figure of the escaping thief had vanished in the thick curtain of smoke hanging over the street.

"He must have gone *that* way," continued Joe grimly. "I'll find him if it's the last thing I do. Wonder where Frank went."

At this instant came a splintering crash near him, followed by a loud yell. Joe squinted through the smoke. The front of a large automobile was jutting through the display window of a small confectionery store!

"Is anybody hurt?" Joe cried, racing over to the wreck. At first the boy saw no one. He yanked open the shop door and went inside. "Gordon!" he gasped in fresh surprise.

Gaping at him from behind a counter littered with shattered glass was the fugitive. The man's shifty eyes darted to and fro, then without warning he lunged directly toward Joe. The lad braced himself, but Gordon was the stronger. Flinging the boy aside, he dashed from the store.

For an instant Joe hesitated. Should he race after the thief, or should he investigate the present scene? Perhaps someone had just been hurt!

A glance through the shattered display window decided him. There was his brother in the very act of pursuing the fleeing Moe Gordon.

"I guess Frank will get him all right," said Joe to himself. "Now let's see what's going on here."

"Mister! Run fetch a police fellow! My shop, she is done for!" came a shrill voice close at hand.

As the smoke and dust cleared gradually from the interior of the tiny shop Joe saw a small, beady-eyed man with a pointed goatee beckoning to him from a corner of the room.

"Are you hurt?" the younger Hardy lad inquired, looking at the agitated fellow anxiously.

"No matter about me. Look at my shop! The big sedan—she run right through the window! Oh, oh, she is owing me ten thousand dollars' damages!"

Moaning and wringing his hands the man paced to and fro blinking at the wreckage.

"What about the driver of the car? Where is he? Is he injured?" Joe asked.

He was about to climb through the debris to

make an investigation when the car door opened. A tall, distinguished-looking man, whose clothes were in a state of wild disarray, stepped down. Knocked out momentarily, he had been lying on the seat of the automobile.

"Is anyone hurt? I'm very sorry this happened," he said in a deep voice that wavered somewhat.

"Ah! You are the fellow that ruinated my little shop," screamed the fussy man with the goatee. "You will pay me!"

"Pardon me, sir," Joe interrupted, "but is there anything I can do for you? Are you in need of a doctor?"

"A little scratched but otherwise all right, thank you," replied the newcomer. "This is indeed an unfortunate occurrence. In trying to avoid colliding with a fire engine, I found myself forced off the road. My car went out of control and——"

"And you shall pay me," hissed the unpleasant shopkeeper. "Just look! My window! My counter! My candies! I shall get a lawyer and sue you!"

The tall man's face blanched. "Now, now, my good sir, please calm yourself. The damages shall be paid, of course. I hardly think, however, that they will run into the thousands."

"Ah, that's what *you* think," howled the shopkeeper venomously. "The damages——"

"By the way," interrupted Joe, looking the shopkeeper squarely in the eye, "weren't you sheltering an escaped criminal a few minutes ago? Wasn't that Moe Gordon behind your counter? And isn't he wanted at police head-quarters?"

It was as if Joe had dropped a bombshell. The man's beady eyes took on a look of terror, and sweat poured from his brow. He looked at the tall newcomer, then at Joe.

"There's a prison sentence for anyone har-boring criminals," Joe went on breezily. "Per-haps——"

At that instant he heard his name called. "Joe!" cried a voice. "So here's where you've been."

"Did you get him, Frank?"

"Gordon?" Frank's face fell. "He's gone. We had a fight and he stole my wallet. I man-aged to give him a good thrashing, but he finally got away. Gee, what happened here?"

"This gentleman has just wrecked his car," Joe explained. "The shopkeeper wants thou-sands of dollars' damages." He winked at his brother as he spoke.

"Wasn't Gordon hiding in here?" Frank asked with a sidelong glance at the man with the goatee. "He must have been. I saw him as he was running out."

The tall man stepped up to the shopkeeper. "I think that if you will give me your name, the matter of damages can be arranged," he said.

"I am Charlie Hinchman," snapped the

other. "And you will pay me. Your name?"

"I am Arthur Barker, president of the Liberty Company. You can reach me there."

With an exchange of significant glances the brothers followed Mr. Barker outside.

"Can we take you anywhere?" Joe offered. "Our car is down the street. We have some things to tell you."

Barker looked at them in mild surprise. "Indeed? Very well, let us go down to my office. I should be grateful for the ride. First, I'll identify myself to the authorities and arrange for the disposition of my car."

He spoke to a policeman, called a garage, then joined the boys. They plunged through the crowd which had collected, finally getting to the Hardy car half a block away. Frank started the engine and quickly drove off.

"I'm afraid that fellow Hinchman is going to make plenty of trouble for me," Barker said, worried. "You can see the type of man he is."

"Perhaps we can help you," Frank declared. "You see, we had a little adventure last night that had something to do with your company."

While the man listened the boys related how they had recovered the stolen cases of valuable silver pieces.

"Mighty fine work!" he exclaimed as they continued. "Goodness, I hadn't heard a thing about it. So you are the Hardy boys, eh? Your father's name is well known. Well, here we are. Let's go into my office and complete this story."

Tom Klip was on hand to greet them. Excitedly, the driver repeated the boys' tale. "And the boxes are here safe, Mr. Barker, in the warehouse."

"But we still haven't caught Gordon," Frank said mournfully. "It's all my fault that we haven't. I shouldn't have let him get away from me."

"Shucks, you couldn't help it," said Joe consolingly. "We'll get him sooner or later."

"If you need any help from me, don't hesitate to let me know," Mr. Barker offered warmly. "Have you any plans as to how to capture him?"

Frank glanced at his brother. "I think we'll go back to Hinchman's shop, Mr. Barker. Maybe we can pick up a clue there. We'll let you know."

As they drove away, Joe spoke up. "If you could have seen Hinchman's face when I started talking about Gordon, Frank! I'll bet those two are in league."

"I *did* see his expression when *I* mentioned Gordon, Joe. But maybe he was just worried about getting money out of Barker for damages."

"*Extra* money, you mean," Joe smiled. "Well, maybe he was. But I've a hunch there's something more to it than that. Why was Gordon hiding in the shop in the first place?"

"He might have run in there because it was the handiest place," suggested Frank.

"Maybe so. Well, here we are. Look, the crowd's bigger than ever. There's the wrecker taking Mr. Barker's car away."

After parking, the boys hurried toward the throng. Once again they could hear Hinchman's raucous voice above everything, shrieking:

"Get away from my shop, the whole kit-and-kiboodle of you! And stop stealing my candies, you dratted kids!"

Joe suppressed a snicker. "Look, Frank, every youngster in the neighborhood is helping himself to that spilled candy. Boy, is that man mad!"

"All right, get away from the store, everybody," rang out the voice of a police officer.

He strode through the crowd and the onlookers gradually dispersed.

"Shall we see if we can make Hinchman talk about Gordon?" suggested Joe.

Frank shook his head. "If he knows anything about the thief he certainly won't tell us about it."

"Listen, Frank, if those two really are in league, they'll be in communication sooner or later. For one thing, Gordon will want to know who are after him and where they're looking."

"You're probably right but that doesn't help any. Unless——"

"Unless we keep a close watch on Hinchman night and day," said Joe.

His brother nodded thoughtfully. "I guess

that would be our best bet, at least for the time being. We'll have to be careful, though, that Hinchman doesn't spot us.''

"I tell you what, Frank. See that vacant store diagonally across the street from Hinchman's? There's an alley next to it. Let's hide there and keep watch.''

It was a tedious assignment. The brothers relieved each other only long enough to get a light repast. The shopkeeper spent the entire day superintending several carpenters in the repair of the damage. Finally, as the boys were about to give up in weary disgust, the workmen went away. The proprietor's wiry form was silhouetted against a light deep in the interior of the partly repaired shop.

"Now's our chance,'' Frank whispered. "Let's get closer and see what he's up to.''

Stealthily they stole across the street in the gathering dusk and approached the store. Frank nudged his brother. "He's talking to somebody, Joe! I thought he was alone.''

The brothers crept to the edge of the broken display window. Cautiously Joe leaned over and peeped inside.

"He *is* alone, Frank! He's talking on the phone! Listen!''

The muffled tones of the shopkeeper drifted out to them. At first they could distinguish none of the words, then a startling sentence came to their ears.

"No, no, Gordon, don't come here tonight,''

Hinchman was saying. He was speaking in a low tone of voice with no rasp in it. "The police will catch you sure. What's that? The two Hardy brats?" The rest of the conversation died away in the sound made by a passing automobile.

CHAPTER V

As THE noise of the passing car faded away the boys could hear Hinchman's voice again. Tense with excitement, they leaned as close to the broken window as they dared.

"What's that?" the proprietor hissed into the telephone. "Does anyone suspect *me?* The police? No! Everybody thinks just what I want them to think—that this is a candy store and I am the dumb shopkeeper. Hah!"

They could hear a sharp *crack* as Hinchman slapped his thigh in an explosion of laughter. Then came a long silence, finally followed by the man's voice again.

"Yes, it's too bad you didn't get away with the Liberty Company boxes, Gordon. But never mind. Next time we'll do better. So long as nobody knows this little candy store is the headquarters for our trucking business! Ha, some joke, eh? Listen, Gordon, I'll tell you something——"

The boys exchanged triumphant looks as Hinchman's voice sank to an inaudible whisper. "Guess we really have something to report to Dad now!" smiled Joe.

"I'll say we have. Come on, we'd better not lose any time. We'll phone him right away."

Together the boys raced down the street and jumped into their car. Five minutes later they hurried into the railroad station where there was a public telephone booth.

"Hello, Dad!" said Frank excitedly a few moments later. "We've traced the trucking gang to their den. No, we'd better not say any more on the phone. Can you come to Aberdeen right away? First thing in the morning? Fine! We'll be at the Lenox Hotel," decided the boy quickly.

The brothers hardly slept, so eager were they to tell their father of the developments in the case.

"What time is Dad's train due?" Joe queried as they dressed shortly after dawn.

"Six-thirty. We'll just about have time to grab a bite of breakfast and get to the station."

Their faces wreathed in grins, the boys greeted their famous father as he stepped off the train.

"So you really have accomplished something, boys? That's fine. Let's go back to your hotel and talk it over," he suggested.

During the next hour the brothers related in detail everything that had transpired since they had left Bayport. From their father's expression it was evident to them that their work met with his positive approval.

"The question is, what shall we do next,

Dad?" Frank asked, as they finished their story.

"You two wait here till I come back," advised Mr. Hardy. "I think I'll have a little chat with Hinchman."

The detective put on his hat and stalked off in the direction Frank indicated. A few minutes later he stood nonchalantly peering through the broken display window of the confectionery shop.

"I see you've had an accident," he drawled, eyeing a small, ferret-like individual who was stooping behind a counter.

"Eh? What's that?" The man looked up with a start. Seeing an apparent stranger he broke into an unpleasant chuckle. "Oh, yes, I have accident, all right. A man drives his big sedan truck into my poor little store. But he shall pay!"

The detective casually walked inside and gazed around. "Nice, cozy little spot you have here. I suppose you'll have it completely fixed up?"

Hinchman's beady eyes surveyed Fenton Hardy suspiciously. "I am having it fixed already. The carpenters, they are coming back at ten o'clock. Are you a stranger in town, Mister?"

Mr. Hardy shrugged his shoulders. "I'm interested in the possible purchase of a small store, to run as a sort of hobby."

The shopkeeper's eyes suddenly gleamed.

"Ah! You are a man after my own heart, Mister. I do the same. My little candy store is my hobby. It is good to have a hobby, yes?"

The detective's face was inscrutable. "You have some other business, then?"

"Ah, yes. I am really a—a truck—a mover. My moving business is at Carside. When I get too tired from that I come over and run my place here."

Mr. Hardy gazed about a moment. "You wouldn't be interested in selling your store to a man who wants a hobby, would you?" he asked casually.

Hinchman cocked his head to one side. "Oh, no, Mister. It is my—my hobby. I do not want to sell."

The detective eyed the other levelly. "Not even for a—a considerable price?"

"Ah, well, perhaps we can get together, Mister. Naturally I do not wish to sell. But at a price—well!" He shrugged. "What do you think my fine business is worth, Mister?"

"I'd have to think it over," said the detective. "First I must know whether you might be willing to part with it."

He started toward the door. Hinchman scurried after him.

"You make me a fair proposition, Mister and the store is yours! Just a fair price, Mister, that's all I ask."

"Thank you. I'll think it over and let you know."

Leaving the shopkeeper staring uncertainly after him Fenton Hardy sauntered away. Hardly had he gone out of earshot, than Hinchman looked up with a start. Someone was pounding on the back door. There were three knocks, then one knock, then three more knocks.

"Ah! It is Matty Storch. Wonder what he wants?" he said half-aloud, going to the rear of the store and turning a key.

"It's about time you let me in, Charlie," came a whisper, as a slender young man with ugly features slipped inside. "I've been tapping our code for ten minutes."

"Oh, I'm sorry. I had a—a customer in the shop, Matty. Don't be mad. What's the trouble?"

"You'll have another customer in the shop pretty soon if you're not careful. Fenton Hardy's in town!"

"Hardy? Fenton Hardy?"

"Yes, Fenton Hardy, the detective! I saw him at the station this morning. Came in on the six-thirty train. Better watch out, Charlie. We don't want to get tangled with that fellow."

The shopkeeper's eyes popped. "What does he look like, Matty? Is he big and tall? Has he got gray hair? Did he wear a gray hat?"

The ugly young man nodded vigorously. "That's the fellow, all right. Why? Say, what's ailing you?"

Hinchman was running up and down, wringing his hands and groaning. "Oh, my! Oh,

my! Matty, everything is lost! Oh, my, why
am I so dumb!"

The young man was staring openmouthed at
the distraught shopkeeper. "Say, what's this
all about? Did you see Hardy? Tell me!"

Hinchman suddenly stopped his pacing.
"Listen, Matty. This morning I was standing
here behind my counter. A man comes along
and looks in the window——"

Two blocks away in the Hotel Lenox another
whispered conference was taking place.

"There's no doubt about Hinchman being in
league with the trucking thieves," Fenton
Hardy was saying to his sons. "And the candy
store, of course, is a cover-up."

He described his interview with the shopkeeper while the boys listened eagerly.

"I think, though, that we'd better proceed
carefully," the detective continued. "In the
first place, the matter of damages should be
settled between Barker and Hinchman. With
that out of the way our work will be easier."

"Then let's go right over and see Mr. Barker," Frank suggested. "He should be in his
office now."

Half an hour later they were seated around
the desk of the distinguished-looking executive.
The boys had introduced their father and had
informed Mr. Barker of their suspicions con-
cerning Hinchman.

"I certainly shall cooperate with you in

every way possible," said the man after hearing their story. "The trucking thieves must be stopped at all costs, of course. I agree with you that, in the meantime, a damage settlement must be made with Hinchman as our first step." He pressed a buzzer and a young woman appeared. "Miss Weed, please phone Mr. Hinchman and ask him if he will be so kind as to come here this evening at eight. Tell him I shall discuss payment for damages at that time."

The secretary disappeared. In the brief silence that followed Frank and Joe gazed wide-eyed at a veritable mass of relics on display in the room. Mr. Barker smiled.

"Yes, boys, those are pieces I've picked up here and there on my travels abroad. That vase came from Siam. That teakwood chair I bought in India. My special hobby is collecting swords, though. I have a great many of them at my home. I'd like to show them to you."

The brothers said they certainly would like to see them.

"What about this sheathed sword, Mr. Barker?" Joe asked, pointing to an old weapon hanging over the president's desk. "Golly, it's a huge thing."

"That," said Mr. Barker, "is my pride and joy. It is a broadsword used by a Crusader during the Holy Wars in the Middle Ages. His name is engraved on the blade and the family coat-of-arms is on the hilt. I found the sword in a small out-of-the-way shop in Europe."

At this moment the secretary returned. "Mr. Hinchman says eight o'clock will be all right," she said. "He promised to be here on the dot."

Fenton Hardy stood up. "In that event I think I shall do some other work for the present and wait till I hear what is decided between yourself and the shopkeeper."

"Very good, Mr. Hardy," returned the executive. "I'll have a chat with the man, offer him what I consider to be fair payment, and see how he acts. As soon as he leaves I'll phone you. That should be about nine o'clock."

As he noticed the boys again looking at the sword, Mr. Barker asked if they would like to see his collection of them right then. "I'm going home to a late luncheon," he said. "Suppose you come along and eat with me. Then I'll show you my treasures," he added.

Frank and Joe were delighted with the invitation. Mr. Hardy declined, but his sons accompanied the man to his car and rode toward his home. They found their host to be a delightful person, full of interesting stories of the Crusaders and other ancient warriors.

"You know," he smiled, "our own soldiers are a bit like the old knights who rode forth encased in armor. Only today the fiery steeds are engines and the armor is steel tanks!"

In a few minutes the boys found themselves driving through the gates of a beautiful estate. Large trees shaded a vine-covered brick mansion. The interior of the house was richly furnished with hangings and rugs as fine as museum pieces.

"My father also was a collector," said Mr. Barker in explanation. "Many of the things you see here belonged to him. He traced his ancestry back many generations and enjoyed trying to find articles belonging to his forebears. We think the knight whose name is on the sword in my office was an ancestor of ours."

"Then that makes the weapon doubly valuable to you, doesn't it?" suggested Frank.

"Yes," agreed the owner. "I should hate to lose it or have anything happen to it."

Luncheon was announced by a butler. The boys, who had had an early breakfast, were very hungry and greatly enjoyed the meal. Their host encouraged them to tell him of their adventures. Though modest about their exploits, the boys told enough for him to realize they were capable of undertaking to solve almost any mystery.

"*My* young days were not so exciting," he smiled. "Well, come along," he added, rising from the table. "Now I'll show you my collection of swords. *They* represent mystery and excitement of several ages ago."

"I almost wish I had lived then," sighed Joe.

If the boys had tried to guess ahead of time the number of pieces on display they would have failed by several hundred. When Mr. Barker opened a door to a large room, Frank and Joe were astounded. Before their eyes were four walls covered solidly with every type of sword known to a collector. Some were several feet long, others only inches in length. Among them were both dull and shiny weapons, with wide or narrow blades, depending upon their use.

The hilts fascinated the boys. Several had coats-of-arms on them, others were plain with a holy cross embossed on the metal. A few were studded with jewels.

"This exhibition is marvelous!" cried Joe. "It would take days to study these swords carefully."

"You're right," agreed Mr. Barker, "and I want you to come again some time. But before we leave, I must show you my most precious collection. It's in that cabinet in the corner."

He preceded Frank and Joe, opening the door to a high massive chest made of oak. Within hung rows of short, exquisitely made weapons, all with precious stones embedded in the hilts.

"These are very rare," explained Mr. Barker. "In fact, I doubt that there is another in the whole world like any one of them. If I were to——"

The man stopped speaking suddenly and a strange look came over his face.

"Is something the matter?" Frank inquired.

"I—I'm afraid I've been robbed!" Mr. Barker replied in a tone which implied he could not believe his own words.

CHAPTER VI

THE BROKEN BLADE

The Hardy boys were shocked to hear Mr. Barker's words. They expressed their sympathy, then inquired what had been stolen.

"A very valuable and unusual sword," the man answered. "It was used long ago by a matador in bullfights. He must have been a great favorite, for this estoque—that's the name of the matador's sword—is unusually attractive. It must have been presented to him by a very wealthy person; perhaps a king or queen."

"Why should anyone steal just that particular sword?" Joe asked. "Others here surely are just as valuable."

"I can't imagine why," said Mr. Barker. "Perhaps the thief planned to take more but was frightened away. This room hasn't been locked for some time, but from now on it will be!"

He strode ahead of the boys into the hall and summoned the butler. After telling the man what had happened, he asked that the key to the museum be brought to him.

"And you recall seeing or hearing no stranger around here at any time lately?" he inquired of the servant.

"No sir," the butler replied. "And I haven't been away from the house for a week," he added, leaving the room to get the key his employer wished.

Frank and Joe asked if there was anything they could do in regard to the mystery of the stolen estoque.

"Thank you, no," said Mr. Barker. "I'll notify the police, but I presume that finding the weapon will be like hunting for a needle in a haystack. But maybe a good detective—why, I had forgotten entirely for the moment."

"Forgotten what, Mr. Barker?" Joe inquired.

"That you boys have solved so many mysteries!" he smiled. "How would you like to find my estoque for me?"

"I'd like nothing better!" cried Frank.

"Just give me a chance!" echoed Joe.

So it was settled that the police would not be notified until the Hardy boys had had a chance to locate the valuable stolen weapon.

"May we stay here for a while this afternoon and start work?" Joe asked excitedly.

"Yes indeed," replied Mr. Barker. "But don't begin by being suspicious of the servants. All of them have been here many years and are entirely trustworthy. Well, I must get back to the Liberty Company now. Good luck in your work."

After the man had gone the boys started their investigation. After a two hour search they gave up. Not one piece of evidence had come to light.

"The thief certainly covered his tracks well," sighed Frank, discouraged. "I guess this case will be one to be solved by headwork rather than footwork."

"Maybe you're right," agreed his brother, "so let's start figuring the solution by guesswork. Idea Number One: maybe the estoque is in some pawnshop."

"Idea Two: it may have been sold to a collector," offered Frank. "Or Number Three: the weapon may have been stolen for some sinister use."

"Like stabbing a bull?" grinned Joe.

"I wish it might be as unimportant as that," said his brother. "But I'm afraid we may pick up the paper some morning and find a story about——"

"Wow, you give me the shivers, Frank. Let's talk about something cheerful," pleaded Joe. "Say, we'd better get back to the hotel. Dad will wonder where we've been all afternoon."

Their father had not known of his sons' long absence, for he had been busy gathering some useful data about valuable shipments of cargo. Upon meeting Frank and Joe he heard the story of the stolen matador's sword with great interest. He thought it a most unusual theft.

"I hope you find the estoque, boys," he said encouragingly. "And one little tip. Look among your bullfighters for the thief."

The eyes of the two young Hardys opened wide. They gazed at their father in admiration.

"We never thought of that!" admitted Frank.

"There aren't any matadors in this country," groaned Joe. "We can't go skipping off to this land and that hunting up bullfighters! What'll we do?"

The detective smiled. "Don't give up so easily," he counseled his sons. "You may get a clue unexpectedly. In the meantime, let's plug at this mystery of the cargo thieves, and more especially on Gordon and Hinchman."

The three Hardys discussed the day's events at the evening meal, but decided to draw no conclusions yet. They would await word of the outcome of the interview to be held at the Liberty Company.

"Golly, I didn't realize it was this late," Joe exclaimed suddenly, looking at his watch after dinner. "It's past eight-thirty already."

"Then we haven't long to wait to hear from Mr. Barker," said his brother with quickening pulse. "He will call us from his office most any time. Say, wasn't that a wonderful sword he had hanging on the wall over his desk?"

"I'd hate to get stuck with it," Joe laughed. "There wouldn't be much left of a fellow!"

"Excuse me, are you Mr. Hardy?" interrupted a voice close to the detective.

It was a bellhop who had approached the trio where they now sat talking in the lobby. "I have a phone call for you, sir."

With a significant look at his sons the detective arose and followed the boy to the telephone booth. A moment later he returned. The brothers sprang from their chairs at sight of their father's expression.

"We must move fast, boys," the detective said in a tense whisper. "It was Miss Weed on the phone. She's very hysterical. Asked us to come to the factory at once."

"What do you suppose has happened?" Joe queried as all three dashed outside to the boys' car.

"We'll know soon," said Frank grimly.

The engine spurted into life and they started down the street.

"Miss Weed didn't say so, but I fear Mr. Barker has met with an accident," Mr. Hardy remarked. "Look, isn't that the Liberty Company straight ahead?"

"There's an ambulance in front of it, Dad!" his younger son exclaimed.

Then came the wail of a siren. Just as Frank nosed their car to a stop along the curb the ambulance clamored past them. Jumping to the sidewalk, the Hardys ran to a familiar figure standing in the doorway of the building.

"Oh, I'm so glad you've come!" cried Miss

Weed. "Something terrible has happened to Mr. Barker! Oh, dear, I hope—I hope——"

"There, there, try to calm yourself," said the detective gently. He took the girl by the arm. "Come inside, Miss Weed, and let me get you a drink of water. Then perhaps you can tell us exactly what happened."

The young woman sank back into a chair, white as a ghost. Joe went in search of a water cooler and reappeared a moment later with a paper cup in his hand.

"Oh, thank you," gasped the secretary, taking the cup. "I—I feel better now."

Sympathetically the boys and their father waited. "I—I left the office late," Miss Weed explained, making an obvious effort to control her emotions. "Mr. Barker was still here, for as you know he had an appointment with Mr. Hinchman."

Mr. Hardy nodded. "Yes. Please continue."

"Upon reaching home I suddenly remembered that I had left some money lying on my desk. It should have been locked in the safe. So I returned immediately, and—and—" she stopped, convulsed by sobs.

"Please, Miss Weed. What happened then?" Mr. Hardy urged gently.

"I opened the office door and—and there was Mr. Barker lying on the floor! The money I had come to get was gone, and the safe door stood wide open."

"Were there any marks of violence on Mr. Barker?" Fenton Hardy asked.

"I—I didn't see any, but—oh, I don't know," moaned the distraught woman. "I called the ambulance right away. Oh, dear, I shall never forget that terrible sight. Poor Mr. Barker!"

Mr. Hardy at length prevailed upon Miss Weed to return to her home. "We shall take care of the situation," the detective comforted her. "You go to bed and try not to worry. Everything, I'm sure, will come out all right."

With a grateful look the young secretary left, whereupon Joe burst into an excited whisper. "Dad, the Crusader's sword is gone from where it was hanging over Mr. Barker's desk!"

"Here's part of it," came Frank's muffled voice from behind a large chair in a corner of the room.

He bobbed up, displaying the hilt of the ancient weapon but only part of the blade.

"Most of the blade is gone!" Joe cried. "See how shiny the jagged edge is? Now, who do you suppose could have done that—and why?"

At that moment there came a pounding at the entrance. Looking up with a start, Fenton Hardy crossed the room and yanked open the door. "Telegram, sir," piped a voice. "For Mr. Barker."

"I'll take it," said the detective. "Here, boy." He flipped the messenger a coin, then shut the door and turned the key.

"Are you going to read it, Dad?" Frank queried.

"Under the circumstances I think we would be justified in doing so," replied the boy's father. "Hmm. It's from Hinchman.

'REGRET CANNOT CALL THIS EVENING STOP MUST GO OUT OF TOWN ON BUSINESS STOP WILL PREFER CHARGES LATER DATE'

Well, that adds a new angle to our little mystery."

The boys looked at each other, mystified. "I wouldn't trust that fellow Hinchman as far as I can throw a stone," said Joe. "He's up to some mischief. There's no doubt about that."

"On the other hand, if he had anything to do with this attack on Mr. Barker, why would he have sent a telegram?" Frank speculated. "That sounds as if——"

"Sounds as if he wanted to make it look as though he didn't know anything about what happened to Mr. Barker," his brother replied. "What do you think, Dad?"

"I think it's time we take some action, boys."

CHAPTER VII

"Joe, there must be a night watchman around," said Fenton Hardy. "Go hunt him up and see what he knows. Meanwhile I'll call the hospital." As the boy departed the detective turned to the phone.

"Any news?" Frank asked eagerly as his father finished speaking.

"None," announced the detective. "The hospital authorities refuse to give out any information except to say that Mr. Barker is in no condition to be questioned."

Joe returned to the room with a disappointing report. "I found the watchman in one of the other buildings. He said he didn't know a thing about what had happened to Mr. Barker."

For several moments there was silence. Finally Mr. Hardy spoke. "Boys, I think you may as well go back to the hotel and get some sleep. I'll scout around and you can take up where I leave off first thing in the morning."

Reluctantly the brothers returned to the Lenox. For a long time they talked, discussing every angle of this new mystery. Was it possible there was any connection between the broken Crusader's sword and the stolen matador's estoque? Had the same person wanted both?

"Mr. Barker owned the two weapons," said Frank. "And on this second occasion the thief may have attacked him because he tried to ward him off."

"Could that person have been Hinchman?"

There seemed to be no answer to the puzzle, and finally, from sheer weariness, the boys fell asleep.

"What's that? Who's there?" Frank sat bolt upright in bed.

To his surprise the sun was streaming into the room. It was morning and someone was knocking at the door. He jumped from bed and hurried to open it.

"Good morning, boys," boomed a hearty voice. "Time for work. It's nearly eight o'clock. Why, I've been all the way home to get my car."

Joe rubbed his eyes ruefully. "Golly, and we were going to get up at five. Dad, what's new?"

"Hinchman's gone! His shop is empty and boarded up."

"W-what?" exclaimed his sons.

Mr. Hardy nodded. "He was too quick for us. We should have kept a closer watch on the man. But there's still a chance. I want you boys to go to Carside right away."

The brothers already were dressing. Joe

rang for breakfast to be sent up immediately.

"What shall we do there, Dad?" he asked.

"Hinchman told me that he had a moving business at Carside. You and I know, of course, what sort of business it is. If it's really at Carside, that's where we ought to be."

"Do you think Hinchman was speaking the truth?" asked Frank.

"There's no telling. He may have spoken without thinking. He didn't know I was a detective when we were talking. Anyhow, we'll take that chance. Now, one more thing."

"Yes, Dad," said Frank expectantly.

"I've checked on freight shipments. There's a big one of new weapons for the government —very valuable—due in Carside some time to-day. I want you boys to watch at the junction for it. You may see Hinchman, or perhaps Gordon."

"We'll be there," Frank promised, starting to eat the breakfast that had just been brought in.

Twenty minutes later the boys waved a cheery farewell to their parent and nosed their car toward the highway. They decided to go past Hinchman's shop.

"There it is, Frank. Completely boarded up, just as Dad said."

"Say, who's that young fellow standing there on the corner? I know him, but I can't place him."

"It's that messenger who brought the telegram last night to Mr. Barker's office," exclaimed Joe.

"You're right. Do you suppose he knows anything about Hinchman?"

"Probably not. He's just a kid. Still, we might talk to him. Won't do any harm."

They parked their car and casually sauntered over to the lad.

"Hello there, young fellow," Joe called pleasantly. "Say, can you tell us anything about this candy store? Seems to have gone out of business."

The messenger boy apparently did not recognize them. "Oh, that! Guess Hinchman— that's the person who owns it—got scared. He heard the big-shot detective was in town."

"Big-shot detective?" Joe blinked innocently.

"Sure. Ain't you heard? Fenton Hardy's in town. Gosh, I wish I could meet him. He's famous!"

The boys tried hard to suppress their smiles, as Frank asked, "What difference does that make to Mr. Hinchman?"

The boy frowned. "Everybody thinks he just runs a candy store, but I know different. He's in with Matty Storch. Matty told him Mr. Hardy was in town, so they both ran away."

"Who's Matty?" queried Joe, rapidly growing tense with suppressed eagerness.

"Oh, he's a fellow who loafs around Hinchman's store. I don't know what they're up to, but they always have a lot of money. I know, 'cause Matty shows me.''

The brothers exchanged significant glances, then Joe asked, "When did Mr. Hinchman leave town? He was here yesterday, because we saw him."

"Oh, he didn't leave till late last night. I watched them go. And Matty showed me an extra big roll of bills. Golly, I sure wish I could find out where Mr. Hardy is. I been lookin' for him all over town ever since breakfast."

Frank pulled his brother aside, his eyes glowing. "Say, Dad ought to know about this," he said. "Let's write him a note before we leave and let this boy take it over."

"Sure thing. Here's a pencil and some paper."

Hastily the younger lad wrote a note of introduction, telling his father the messenger had an interesting story to relate. In the meantime Frank asked the lad guardedly if Hinchman or Storch were interested in weapons, either new or old.

"I dunno. I don't think so," replied the urchin. "Leastwise I never saw any or heard 'em say anything about old ones. Course each of 'em has a gun."

"I see," said Frank. "Well, how would you like to earn some money? Will you deliver this note to Mr. Hardy at the Lenox Hotel?"

"Mister H-H-Hardy? You mean the famous detective? Are you sure you ain't kiddin'?" The boy's eyes were round with wonder as he spoke.

"We're not kidding," Joe laughed. "Here's the message. Take it over right away and wait until he reads it. He'll pay you."

"Whoops! Thanks, fellows! I'll be seein' ya!" Like a shot the lad was off. For a moment Frank and Joe stood smiling.

"Well, let's move on," suggested the former. "We've plenty to do and Carside's a good sixty miles from here."

A long detour delayed them and by noontime they still had several miles to go. Speed was impossible over the rough, narrow road. Huge clouds were piling up ominously overhead, blotting out the sun, and there was a fierce gale blowing.

"If the rain comes, this road will be a river," Frank observed. "Wow! There it is!"

There was a sudden rat-tat-tat on the car roof as the deluge fell. In a short time it was impossible to see more than ten feet ahead. Lightning illuminated the road, where huge tree limbs were whipping to and fro. Suddenly there was a blinding flash, followed instantly by a splintering sound.

"It's a tree, Frank, right ahead! It's coming down! Back the car up, quick!"

In a flash Frank had the wheels in reverse.

The auto gathered momentum as if some huge, unseen hand were pushing it.

"We're sliding off the road," cried Joe, clutching his brother's arm. "Look! We're right over a precipice!"

At that instant the giant tree in front of the boys crashed to the ground, missing them by inches, and flinging twigs and mud in all directions. The Hardys scarcely noticed the narrowness of their escape from that quarter, however, for the other situation looked more desperate to them.

"Jump out, Joe!" Frank cried. "Quick, it's our only chance."

It was too late. With a shudder the car slipped backward over the precipice. Instinctively the boys braced themselves for the crash that seemed inevitable.

"W-why, what happened?" Joe suddenly cried.

The auto seemed to have come to a complete standstill in mid-air. Gingerly Frank stuck his head out and peered around.

"We're suspended on a clump of branches, Joe! There's a tree jutting right out from a crevice in the rock."

Cautiously Joe leaned over his brother's shoulder and looked down. The car was tilted at a crazy angle. "One little slip and we'll plunge a hundred feet. Those branches are likely to crack any minute."

"We must climb out!" urged Joe.

Gingerly his brother opened the door and stepped to the running board.

"If we can crawl along this big limb to the end, we'll be able to shin up the rocks," he called.

On all fours the boys slowly made their way. The rain stung their faces like pointed darts. The gale threatened to tear them loose and fling them onto the rocks below. Grimly they hung on.

At last Frank reached the side of the precipice. "You all right, Joe?" he called.

"Yes. Go ahead."

Frank swung himself to the top of the cliff. In a jiffy his brother followed suit.

"Golly, that was about as close a call as a fellow'd ever want," Joe muttered. "Wonder how soon our faithful old bus will fall?"

"Any minute, I'm afraid. We're going to have a long walk."

The unmistakable clatter of a motor sounded above the noise of the storm. The boys looked up. Could they believe their eyes? Yes, there was a powerful wrecking car swinging around the corner toward them.

"Hey, Mister," Joe called, running out into the road and waving. "Stop!"

"Hello, there! What's the trouble?" boomed a genial voice from the driver's cab. "Oh, so you've gone over the cliff. I guess I can get you out before I go on. Somebody up the line phoned he's stuck in the mud."

"We're in luck," Joe whispered exultantly to his brother. "Maybe we'll get to Carside in time for that freight shipment after all."

The wrecking car driver meanwhile had been looking at their machine. "If we can get a rope around her axle we'll be all right," he said.

Sloshing around in the mud, the boys worked rapidly under the man's direction. Frank crawled down the face of the cliff, and snubbed the rope onto their car. In a moment he was back on the road again.

"You oughta be a circus acrobat, young fellow," commented the driver with a grin.

There was a prolonged grinding sound as the wrecking car backed away, pulling the automobile over the top of the precipice.

"That's too good to be true, Frank! I never thought we'd sit in the old bus again," cried Joe.

"Our troubles are only half over," said Frank. "We have to get that big tree off the road if we're going on to Carside."

"Guess we can tow that thing out of the way in no time," decided the wrecking-car driver. "You boys mind lending me a hand?"

For several moments the three worked hard, attaching ropes and chains to various parts of the huge trunk.

"How far is it to Carside?" Frank asked the driver.

"About two miles, straight ahead."

"Is there an army encampment or government warehouse in this vicinity?'' inquired Joe.

''There is a warehouse,'' the man replied. ''About three miles from here. The government's got all sorts of stuff parked away there, I'm told. Got that cable fastened?'' he called to Frank.

''Yes,'' the boy replied. ''Let her go.''

Once again the powerful wrecker started. With a loud groan and a splintering sound the huge, lightning-stricken tree was moved to the side of the road. Quickly the boys untied the cables, thanked the man for his help, and paid him for rescuing their car.

''Do you know whether the government has trucks to haul away all its shipments that come in on the railroad?'' asked Joe. ''Or does some private company do it?''

''I believe the warehouse has some trucks of its own,'' the man responded, ''but when there's a big shipment, the government hires the Ace Line to help them out. Well, so long, fellows. Hope you make town all right.''

As the boys climbed into their car, Frank said, ''And *I* hope our bus is all right. Yes,'' he added, as the car started and moved along the road, ''the accident didn't hurt it, thank goodness.''

Nearing town, the boys were forced to stop at an intersection where there was a red light. A truck rumbled up on the road to their right and turned ahead of them. On its side was painted ''Ace Line.''

"Frank!" his brother cried excitedly. "I'll bet that fellow is going to the freight station. Let's follow him."

"Right. It's up to us to find out whether that truck belongs to the Ace Line or to the bunch of thieves."

Eagerly they kept their eyes riveted to the truck ahead. Suddenly it swerved into a side road and came to a stop beside the Carside freight depot. Almost at the same moment a long freight train chugged laboriously into the siding.

"We'd better park here and walk the rest of the way to avoid arousing suspicion," suggested Joe.

Frank stopped the car and the two sauntered toward the station, keeping a sharp lookout for any indication that they might have been recognized. Apparently no one was about except the man they were following. They had never seen him before, and they assumed that he did not know them. They walked to the station platform as if they had no particular purpose in being there.

"Ace Line?" called out a trainman just then, jumping from a box car.

"Right here," said the truckman, a burly fellow. "Got my government shipment? Have to deliver that first thing in the morning."

"Let's see your credentials."

The driver shoved a sheaf of papers into the trainman's hand. "All right, your stuff is in that red car over there, fourth from the end.''

Impatiently the boys watched while the man loaded his truck with the heavy boxes. The task finished, he drove off rapidly. Hastening to their car, the Hardy boys pursued him, though keeping at a discreet distance.

"What do you think, Frank? Is he one of the thieves or is he really the company's driver?"

"That remains to be seen," was the reply.

The truck suddenly turned into a side street and drove into a yard alongside a large building. On an electric sign were the words "Ace Line."

"Another wild goose chase," mourned Joe. "But at least we know the stuff wasn't stolen."

"Let's go back to the freight siding. Perhaps another truck will come," suggested Frank.

As the boys reached the next street a large vehicle roared past them, going at a terrific clip. On its side were the words "Ace Line."

"That's Moe Gordon!" cried Frank. "I'm certain of it!"

"Gordon?" Joe's eyes nearly popped from their sockets. "Then put on the gas! Follow him!"

"He's on his way to the depot, sure as you're alive!" Frank stated.

Grimly the older lad steered his car in and out among the slower-moving vehicles that cluttered the road.

Excitedly Joe squinted into the distance.

"He's getting out to talk with one of the trainmen."

The Hardys rushed on.

"He's getting into his truck again, Frank," Joe's voice rang out in dismay. "He's not coming this way. He's crossing the tracks in the opposite direction."

"We must get him!"

CHAPTER VIII

THERE was a sudden puff of steam ahead. "It's the freight train," groaned Joe. "It's starting up. Better not try to beat it, Frank."

It was too late even to make the attempt. By the time the Hardys approached the crossing they found it blocked.

"Wait a minute," said Joe, and hurried toward the depot. He returned a few minutes later. "Just wanted to check up on something. The station agent says that last fellow who drove up in a truck wanted the government shipment, too!"

"Did the man say anything else about him?"

"Said he'd never seen him before and that the boxes already had been given to an Ace Line driver."

Frank's eyes glowed. "We're on the right track anyhow. So Gordon's trying to steal from the government now. That's a pretty serious offense. Say, what does that fellow over there want?"

A pathetic-looking hobo was approaching them, walking with a decided limp. Though dressed in tattered clothes, he appeared nevertheless to be young and pleasant.

"Hello, fellows! Wonder if you'd mind giving me a lift? I'm pretty hungry and weak. Haven't had a square meal since yesterday."

The boys gazed at the young man sympathetically. "Shall we buy him something to eat, Frank?" whispered Joe.

"He looks as if he needs it," his brother responded. Turning to the man, he said, "Jump in. We'll treat you to lunch."

With a grateful smile the fellow pulled himself into the car. "I sure could eat. Golly, you're the first people who've been decent to me for a long time. But it was my own fault." He paused for several seconds, then added, "I was with a circus, but I fell off a trapeze and have never been the same."

"Have you been—wandering ever since then?" Joe inquired.

"I've been a bum, fellows, and do you know why? Because that fall from the trapeze knocked my brains out. Really! I can't remember a thing that happened to me before that." He lowered his voice and looked at the Hardys beseechingly. "I don't know who I am, fellows. Not even what my name is."

Frank stopped the car at a roadside restaurant, where they went in and ordered food. Between mouthfuls the stranger continued his pathetic tale.

"So I've been tramping around ever since, trying to find out who I am and hoping to locate my family. Some day perhaps I shall find them—'' His eyes filled with tears and he stopped talking.

Frank looked at his brother. ''I think we ought to help this man, Joe, don't you? Maybe Dad could aid him in locating his people.''

''That's an idea, Frank. Let's take him to Aberdeen.''

It was just suppertime when the three walked into the hotel there.

''Dad'll be eating, probably,'' said Joe. ''You two wait here and I'll find him.''

A moment later Fenton Hardy strode into the lobby with Joe. As his eyes rested on the stranger, he stopped short.

''Narris Webster!'' he exclaimed.

''Why, Dad, do you know this man?'' Joe exclaimed.

He glanced at the hobo. There was no sign of recognition on the stranger's part. Meanwhile Mr. Hardy was fumbling in his coat pocket, from which he drew forth a small, worn photograph.

''There he is, boys, and to you goes the credit for having found him.''

''But—but, Dad—'' Frank began wonderingly.

''You have brought with you none other than Narris Webster, nicknamed Narvey, the missing son of Axel Webster, the millionaire!''

The brothers gaped at each other and at their father. As for the hobo, he seemed to be perplexed.

"Where did you get this picture, Dad?" asked Frank.

"I happened to run across it not long ago in the police files. I remember the case well. It was about four years ago, I think, that Narris Webster ran away from home and joined a circus."

The hobo listened with interest but showed no sign that he recalled these facts. Mr. Hardy patted the fellow gently on the shoulder.

"Maybe we'd better sit down while I tell you Narvey's story," he suggested.

Still apparently quite weak, the young man fell gratefully into a near-by chair while the others gathered around him.

"Narvey, you had an unhappy childhood, for your father seemed stern to you, so when you grew up you ran away from home to avoid the harsh discipline imposed upon you."

"I remember nothing of my early life," the young man explained. "You state I am the son of Axel Webster. Am I really? Am I Narris Webster?"

"You are," replied the famous detective gently. "There is no mistaking your identity."

The erstwhile hobo gazed into space for a full minute before speaking. The Hardys waited respectfully. At last he spoke.

"No father would be proud of a son like me," he said. "I believe I better think things over before I go—go home. Anyway, I'll get a job so I can buy some decent clothes."

"It would be pretty hard for you to get a job unless you have suitable clothes," argued Mr. Hardy. "I'll advance you the money for some. Frank! Joe! Help this fellow get a bath and a shave. Then buy him some things to wear."

The detective would not listen to young Webster's plea to wait, so off he went with the boys. Immediately Mr. Hardy put in a long distance telephone call.

"Hello, Mr. Axel Webster? This is Fenton Hardy, the detective. I've found your son!" A loud crackling sounded in the receiver. "No, sir, I assure you this is not a hoax. He is here with me. What's that? You'll get the first plane you can, but that won't be for several hours. Very good, I'll meet you at the airport. Good-bye."

Three blocks away Frank, Joe and Narvey entered a store. In a short time the latter was outfitted and the group returned to the hotel.

"Narvey, you look like a new man," Mr. Hardy beamed. "Well, dinner is almost over but they'll still serve us."

During the meal their guest was very quiet. To avoid further embarrassment to him the others talked on many subjects, purposely avoiding the topic of Mr. Webster, senior. As soon as they had eaten, the detective suggested that Narvey retire immediately.

"You need to gain back your strength," he

said. "And furthermore, tomorrow will be a big day in your life."

"How's that?" asked the young man, looking frightened.

"There's nothing to worry about," Mr. Hardy assured him. "Your father will forgive everything. I talked with him on the phone. He is very eager to see you and will arrive tomorrow morning."

Narvey made no reply. He seemed to be very nervous, but this was natural. After a good night's sleep he would be more composed. He was given a room next to that of the boys.

"If you want anything, just call," said Joe, closing the door.

He went into the next room where Frank and Mr. Hardy were waiting.

"I think Narvey's mind will clear when he gets his strength back," said the detective. "By the way, I'm to meet Mr. Webster at nine o'clock at the airport."

"Golly, won't that be exciting?" Joe exclaimed. "Imagine finding a long-lost son after all these years!"

"Dad, have you heard anything about Mr. Barker?" asked Frank.

"No, son," his father replied. "I'll call the hospital now."

The detective picked up the telephone. After a brief conversation he put down the instrument. "They tell me that he still is in no condition for any questioning," were his words.

"It's a great mystery," Frank said thoughtfully. "And by the way, we haven't done a single thing about solving the mystery of the broken blade or the stolen estoque."

"We haven't had time," replied Joe. "Incidentally, I have a new theory. There's one person we hadn't thought of before as Mr. Barker's attacker."

"Who's that?"

"Moe Gordon! Maybe it was he who came in, held up Mr. Barker, and took his money."

The boy's voice rose as he spoke. Up to now the Hardys' conversation had been only a murmur in the next room. The last words had been heard plainly.

"What was that? Did I hear the name Moe Gordon?" muttered a voice from the bed.

Slowly, like an apparition, the gaunt figure pulled itself upright. Etched over the pallid features was an expression of haunting fear.

"Moe Gordon . . . Moe Gordon . . . I must leave before he finds me . . . !" panted the young man.

Quivering in terror, Narvey pulled on his new clothes.

"They're keeping me here on purpose—so Moe Gordon will find me. They didn't mean all that stuff about me being the son of a millionaire. But I'll fool them! I'll get out!"

Stealthily the fellow crept to the hall door.

It was locked, and there was no key. He tip-toed to the adjoining bathroom.

"The window—it is open," he said to himself. Eagerly, his eyes blazing with an unnatural brilliance, Narvey peered out. "Ah! We're only on the second story. That will make it easy."

Furtively he glanced behind him. Then carefully he crawled out the window onto a narrow ledge which wound around that side of the building.

"There's a fire escape at the corner of the ledge. If I can make that it will be easy to get away before Moe—ouch! My leg!"

Slowly and painfully Narvey inched his way on his precarious perch. Suddenly he stopped. He gave a sharp cry as one foot slipped. A second later the figure had left the ledge.

CHAPTER IX

"WHAT was that sound?" Joe queried suddenly.

"I didn't hear anything," responded Frank.

"It sounded like a yell. Maybe I'd better have a look at Narvey," said his brother, going to the fellow's room. In an instant the boy was back. "He's gone!"

"Better go downstairs and look for him," said the detective, jumping up. "Frank and I will investigate here."

Within a minute the two had concluded the missing fellow had left by the window. As they were leaning out to learn what they could, Joe returned out of breath.

"Narvey has escaped in our car!" he cried. "He whizzed past me just as I was running out of the hotel. Dad, let Frank and me take your automobile and chase him!"

Like a shot the two boys bolted downstairs.

"Which way did he go?" Frank asked, jumping behind the wheel of his father's car.

"Down that street! We'll have to hurry if we hope to catch him!"

Several hours later Fenton Hardy paced his

hotel room restlessly, glancing at his watch every few seconds.

"What on earth is keeping those boys?" he muttered to himself for the tenth time. "Surely they must have caught up with young Narvey by now." He studied his watch again. "Hm. Quarter to twelve," he said aloud.

The detective lay down on the bed but could not sleep. Each time a car went by he hoped his sons were returning. But they did not come back, nor did they send any word. At eight o'clock their father, haggard and worried, went downstairs, told the desk clerk he was going to the airport, and asked him to take any messages.

"This puts me in a mighty embarrassing position. I'll have to keep Axel Webster away as long as possible," were his thoughts.

The detective summoned a cab and rode to the airport. While waiting he called the hotel, only to learn that no one had telephoned him.

"Plane Number Fourteen just coming in," droned a voice over the platform amplifier.

Soon a giant air liner began circling the field. It swooped to a graceful landing.

"That must be Webster," speculated Mr. Hardy, as his keen eyes saw a small, well-dressed elderly man gazing about uncertainly. The detective stepped up to the traveler. "Mr. Axel Webster? I am Fenton Hardy."

"How do you do? Yes, I am Axel Webster. You have news of my son? Are you quite certain it is he?'' The millionaire spoke in crisp, precise tones.

''I have every reason to believe that the young man found by my two boys is Narris Webster. I have here a photograph sent out by the police.''

''Let me see it, please. Yes, that is he. And the young man you have found conforms to the photograph? Exactly?'' He scrutinized Fenton Hardy's face suspiciously. Then he broke into a mirthless laugh. ''You must forgive me if I appear to be skeptical, but I have been fooled many times,'' he explained. ''But, tell me, where is my boy?''

Master of the art of self-control though he was, Mr. Hardy reddened slightly. ''We shall be with him presently, Mr. Webster. You must be tired and hungry after your trip. Shall we have a bite to eat at the airport restaurant before we return to my hotel?''

Webster shrugged impatiently. ''I am interested only in seeing my son, if indeed it is he. I suppose, though, a little food would be a good idea.''

Mr. Hardy led his guest into the restaurant and ordered breakfast for both of them.

''Will you excuse me a moment while I make a phone call?'' asked the detective presently. He disappeared into a booth. ''Hello, is this the Lenox Hotel? This is Mr. Hardy. Any messages? What's that? None?''

With a frown of annoyance the detective went back to the table. Webster regarded him questioningly.

"Is something wrong?" he asked.

"Oh, no," replied the detective, forcing a laugh. "Just a little business matter I had to attend to. Well, this fruit looks good."

"Tell me about your discovery of my son," said Mr. Webster. "How did it all happen? I am eager to know the facts and the details!"

With a long breath the detective began his tale, wondering what sort of ending he would be able to give to it.

"Can you beat that?" Joe was bemoaning far out on the highway. "No gas! Of all times for such a thing to happen! Eleven o'clock at night!"

"Narvey must be miles ahead of us now," added his brother sadly. "Well, there's no use just sitting here. Let's find a gas station and fill up the tank."

"We passed one about three miles back."

Half an hour later, heavy-hearted with disappointment, they trudged into the filling station.

"Out of gas? Sure, I'll fix you up," said the attendant cheerily, "but I can't leave here. I'll give you enough so that you can get started. Then drive your car back to fill up."

There was nothing else to do. By the time

the boys returned to the service station and were ready to start on again, more than an hour had passed.

"We'll never catch Narvey now," thought Frank, as he waited for Joe to wash his hands in the little building. "I'd give up the chase except that he has our car."

At this moment his brother came hurrying outside, a paper booklet in his hands. On its cover were the words "Swords of All Lands."

"Is this yours?" he asked the attendant excitedly.

"No," replied the man. "Some fellow dropped it out of his car. I kept it, thinking he might return for it, but I guess he isn't coming back. Mighty interesting pictures."

Joe had thumbed through the pages quickly and his eye had caught a marked item of great importance to him. He must have the book!

"We're particularly interested in the subject of swords," the boy said. "Especially right now."

The attendant made just the reply for which the lad had hoped. "Why don't you take the book along? Just leave your name, in case the fellow should call for it."

"Did he look like a bullfighter?" asked Joe suddenly.

The question startled the man, but he laughed. "I wouldn't know what he does in his spare time, but when he's working, he drives a truck."

"A truck!" both boys echoed.

The attendant could give them no further information, not even the name on the truck nor an accurate description of the driver. The boys thanked the man and left.

"What do you think I saw in this book?" Joe cried to Frank as they resumed their trip. "A picture of an estoque. In pencil alongside it was written 'Panser Antique Shop, Newton.' That's not far from here."

"It's a clue worth following," said Frank. "So the time we lost hasn't been wasted."

For a long while the boys rode in silence; in fact, until dawn lighted the sky. Coming to a fork in the road, they stopped to consider which way Narvey might have gone. With nothing to guide them, they decided to follow the road leading to Newton. Presently they came to railroad tracks. A freight was just pulling away from a siding.

"Look!" cried Joe suddenly. "There's our car parked over there in the bushes! Quick, pull up alongside! Maybe Narvey's here!"

"There he is," Frank exploded, pointing toward the train. "He's on the platform of the caboose! We must stop him!"

"Let's each take a car and chase the train," said Joe. "When it stops, or if Narvey should jump off, we'll grab him."

"All right. You take Dad's automobile."

In a second both cars were roaring down the road which, fortunately, paralleled the railroad tracks. For several minutes the Hardys kept abreast of the freight train which was proceeding now at a fairly rapid pace.

Suddenly Frank, who was in the lead, held out his hand and signaled Joe to stop. The two cars squealed to a halt in the dust.

"How would it be if I go on ahead to Newton and have the train flagged?" asked Frank.

"Good. I'll keep watch over Narvey. If he should jump off I'll go after him," Joe replied.

Twenty minutes later his brother returned to report that the agent would stop the train. "He didn't like the idea, but I convinced him that it was important," explained Frank.

About a mile from town the road swerved away from the tracks, so that the Hardys were forced to give up their watch of the fugitive. He was still sitting on the back platform of the caboose, however, and did not act as if he had any intention of leaving.

The boys reached the station just as the long freight shivered to a stop. Jumping from their automobiles they raced toward the last car. Narvey was not in sight! Frank dashed in one direction, Joe in another, searching behind buildings, on top of the cars, and on the metal rods underneath them.

"Guess he's gone," sighed Frank as the two brothers met on the platform. "Say, those trainmen look mad."

A few feet away the station agent was exchanging harsh words with the train crew. "I tell you a fellow ordered me to stop the train,'' he was shouting. ''Don't blame me. He said there was a fellow stealing a ride who's wanted by the police. Say, there's the one I talked to!'' he raged.

Several members of the crew crowded around the Hardy boys.

''What's the meaning of all this?'' demanded one of them, catching Frank by his collar.

''It's just as I told the agent,'' replied the lad coolly. ''We're looking for a man who climbed on board near Aberdeen. He's wanted by the police. But I guess he got away.''

The head trainman was furious. ''You young fellows sure are meddlers. Anybody'd think you were detectives! After this mind your own business and don't interfere with the operations of the railroad.''

He shouted an order and the freight train began to move. Chagrined, the boys returned to their cars.

''I hate to report this to Dad,'' said Frank, ''but I'm afraid he'll be worried if we don't phone.''

''Let's wait until eight o'clock,'' suggested Joe. ''No use getting him out of bed. Gee, I could stand a little sleep myself.''

''What say we get some breakfast and then hunt up that antique store?'' said Frank. ''Wouldn't it be great to find the stolen estoque there?''

"Sure would, Joe. We shan't find the missing blade of the Crusader's sword there, though, because nobody would buy such a thing."

"I can hardly wait to talk to Mr. Barker," said his brother, "and ask him the name engraved on the blade. That will be a big help in finding it and clearing up the mystery of what happened in the office that night."

After a good meal the boys called their father, only to be told he had gone out. They decided to leave no message but to telephone later.

"Now for that Mr. Panser's shop. Hope he's open," said Joe. "Well, what is your guess? Do we find the matador's sword or don't we?"

"If we don't, at least I hope we get a clue to where it is," replied his brother. "My hunch is it'll be that way."

He was right. The white-haired shopkeeper told the boys a man had been in there only a few days before trying to sell him such a weapon.

"But I couldn't pay as much as he wanted," said the proprietor. "Anyway, I'm always wary of strangers coming in to sell things. Their wares may have been stolen and that would get me in trouble."

"Will you describe this man?" asked Frank, trying not to show his excitement.

What little the antique dealer could offer might fit any number of people. Other than to learn the fellow was rather heavy-set and dark, the boys gleaned nothing more about his appearance.

"Would you say the man might be a matador?" inquired Joe.

"I shouldn't think so. Not quick enough on his feet. Looked more like a—a strong truck driver. But he did say something about a matador at that. Seems to me he said he'd had a good offer from one of them to buy that estoque."

After leaving Mr. Panser, the boys discussed his information excitedly. They concluded that finding the stolen estoque might not take them out of the country after all; maybe not even out of the state!

"Before we do any more sleuthing, I'll have to take Dad's car to a garage," said Joe. "The brakes need adjusting."

The boys ran the two automobiles to a service station and were told to drive down an alleyway to a back entrance. While a mechanic was at work on their car, they strolled through the building toward the front entrance.

"Frank!" cried Joe suddenly. "Look who's coming in the door. It's Narvey!"

CHAPTER X

BEFORE the millionaire's son could turn about and flee, Joe had caught him by an arm.

"Narvey!" he cried. "Why are you trying to run away from us? We want to help you."

The young man peered at Joe hesitantly. "P-please let me go. Please!" He tried to push the Hardy boy from him.

"What about your father, Narvey?" Frank broke in. "Have you forgotten that he's coming for you this morning?"

"M-my father? Oh, you mean Mr. Webster?"

Frank eyed his brother significantly. "The poor fellow needs a doctor," he remarked in an undertone. Aloud he added, "Won't you come with us, Narvey?"

"You won't send me to jail?" asked the young man plaintively.

"To jail!" exclaimed Frank with a perplexed look. "Who said anything about jail?"

"I did," replied Narvey. "I'm going to be sent to jail. I know it!"

Joe put his arm on the frightened speaker's shoulder. "Narvey, something's bothering you. What is it? Please tell us. We'll do anything we can to help you."

For a moment young Webster studied the boys' faces searchingly, biting his nails nervously as he did so. Finally he drew a deep breath. "Have you caught Moe Gordon yet?" he asked so unexpectedly that the brothers winced in surprise.

"Do you know Moe Gordon?" Frank countered.

"Well, I, uh, yes. I worked for him. Doing odd jobs," Narvey burst forth. "I've tried to get away from Gordon, but he keeps hounding me and threatening to expose me if I don't do what he wants."

"So that's the situation, is it?" said Joe. "Well, Narvey, those men will be taken care of sooner or later. You won't have to worry about yourself. Frank and I will see that no harm comes to you."

"We certainly will," agreed Frank. "And now you'd better return with us. My Dad is probably wondering where we all are."

"I don't know what to do," said Narvey.

After much persuasion the young man finally consented. Joe took him across the street to buy him some breakfast. Frank again telephoned the Lenox, only to be told that Mr. Hardy had not returned. By the time Narvey had eaten, the brakes on Mr. Hardy's car had been adjusted, so the brothers and their guest started for Aberdeen, Narvey traveling with Joe.

"I'll bet Dad has been dreadfully worried,"

said Frank, when they reached the hotel. "I wonder if Mr. Webster has arrived."

As they came to the door of their room, the boys stopped short. From within they could hear a raging voice, crying:

"I'll have the law on you, Hardy. Just what do you mean, getting me here all the way from High Point for—for nothing? It's all a monstrous hoax. I tell you I'll—!" The voice ceased as if it had been cut with a knife. "Narris! My son!" were the man's next words.

The Hardy boys and their companion stood still on the threshold. Mr. Webster hastened across the room and embraced the young man.

"Narris! Don't you remember me? Don't you remember your father? Speak up, Narris!" he pleaded.

The son regarded his old father distantly, then ambled over and fell into a chair. "I'm sorry, but I don't," he said. "I wish somebody would get me a drink of water," he mumbled. "I'm thirsty."

Mr. Webster stared at the young man with sad eyes. "You poor lad," he said. "You're sick. Never mind, I'll take good care of you. Perhaps you had better lie down and rest."

A few moments later Narvey stretched out on the bed and closed his eyes. Mr. Webster looked at him so wistfully that Frank and Joe could hardly keep lumps from their throats.

"Step in here a moment, will you, please?"

the man asked. He had risen and was motioning toward Frank and Mr. Hardy. "You'll stay with Narris, won't you, Joe?"

The other three assembled in an adjoining room. Mr. Webster obviously was striving to control his emotions.

"First let me thank you, Frank, and I include your brother, for the wonderful thing you have done in bringing my son to me. You shall be well rewarded. Now, Narris's mental state is very serious, as you have noticed. We must send for a specialist at once. Is there a reputable one near-by?"

"I am personally acquainted with Doctor Rhodes at Williamsburg," said Mr. Hardy. "I'll be glad to call him for you."

"Please do so at once," replied the millionaire.

Due to his friendship with the doctor and his prominence as a detective, Mr. Hardy was able to get the physician to promise to leave for Aberdeen within an hour. He and the boys met him in the lobby and took the man into a little parlor that they might talk about the case before going upstairs.

"My sons can give you some interesting details you may want to know," said Mr. Hardy.

The brothers related their story, including mention of Moe Gordon.

"Narvey Webster's condition sounds serious, I am sorry to say," said the physician when they had finished. "One thing is certain. For his own peace of mind we shall have to contrive to rid him of all fear of the thief. That is absolutely essential if we are to hope for any kind of improvement in his mental state."

"That may not be so simple," Joe ventured. "The police in forty-eight states would like to rid the country of Gordon and Hinchman, but they're hard to catch."

"Nevertheless we shall try to convince young Webster that he himself has nothing to fear. Well, I'll go upstairs now."

The millionaire greeted the group with an anxious expression. "My son won't sleep and he won't talk," he said excitedly.

"I shall examine him at once," replied the physician.

"We'd better leave the doctor and the Websters to themselves for a while," whispered Mr. Hardy to his sons, so the three went to his room.

As they entered, the telephone rang. The detective answered it. As he replaced the receiver his eyes brightened. "Mr. Barker has been discharged from the hospital," he announced.

"Really?" Joe exclaimed.

"That was he on the phone. He is home and wants me to come right over to see him. He says he wants to tell me what happened in his office that night."

Frank looked at his parent hopefully. "May we go with you, Dad?"

Mr. Hardy shook his head. "I think you boys

had better wait here. You may be needed——"

He motioned toward the next room, from which they could hear the murmur of voices. Frank and Joe nodded understandingly.

Hurrying outside, the detective stepped into his car and settled himself behind the wheel. As he reached the outskirts of the residential area, there was a sudden movement in the back of the automobile.

"Drive straight ahead—and keep your eyes on the road," came a low snarl from behind the detective.

Fenton Hardy stiffened. In the rear-vision mirror he could see a masked face huddled in a corner of the back seat.

"Hurry up! Don't stop!" threatened the voice as the captive lessened his speed.

The detective complied, speculating meanwhile on the identity of the stranger.

"Turn left at the next corner," came the command. "Now head for the highway. Don't look around. Keep your eyes on the road."

They passed along a crowded street.

"Shall I ram something and put a quick stop to this?" thought the detective. "No, that would be foolish. Spoil our chances of locating the rest of the gang. I'll just sit tight and take his confounded orders for a while."

Soon they were rolling down the highway in the direction of Carside.

"Don't you think your little game has gone far enough?" Mr. Hardy asked presently.

"It ain't your place to ask questions, Mr. Big-Shot Detective," growled the unpleasant voice. "Slow down. See that country road over there? Turn into it."

From the smooth highway the car wheeled into a narrow, rutted lane. For several minutes they bounced along. When a small clearing appeared on the right, the stranger barked:

"Turn in there. When you get to the other side, stop and switch off the engine."

The next thing the detective knew a hand of steel had closed around his neck. As he struggled he could hear running footsteps and new voices.

"That ought to fix him, Gordon."

"Matty, what took you so long? You're——"

Something crashed on Mr. Hardy's head and all went black.

CHAPTER XI

At the Lenox Hotel Doctor Rhodes was speaking to the Hardy boys in hushed tones.

"Young Webster's mental condition is serious, as I thought, though not hopeless. I have endeavored to assure him that he has nothing to fear from this Moe Gordon, and as a result his mind seems easier."

"What do you think should be done for him next, Doctor?" Frank queried gravely.

"He must have complete rest. I have suggested that his father take the young man to his childhood home. Good food and happy surroundings will help him more than anything else."

At this moment the millionaire appeared, saying his son was ready to leave. "I suppose, boys, that Doctor Rhodes has told you of our plans. He and I are going to take Narris home on the next plane."

"If there's anything we can do for you—" Frank began, whereupon Mr. Webster smiled broadly.

"You two boys already have performed the greatest possible service for me. You have restored my son to me."

"May we take you to your plane?" Joe asked.

At Mr. Webster's nod of assent he turned toward Narvey's room. The young man seemed cheerful and friendly.

"Will you come to see me some time?" he asked. "I feel that I know you, but Mr. Webster—my father—is like a stranger to me."

The boys promised. At the airport Mr. Webster once again expressed his gratitude to the Hardys. Waving happily, he followed Doctor Rhodes and Narvey into the plane.

"Now we'd better get to work," said Frank. "We've several clues to track down. Wonder if Dad's back."

There was no sign of Fenton Hardy when they returned to the hotel.

"Suppose I call the Barker home," suggested Joe. "Maybe we too can go out there and hear his story." The lad was very excited when he returned to his brother. "Dad never arrived at Mr. Barker's house, and Mr. Barker didn't phone him!" he blurted out.

"Is Mr. Barker home from the hospital?" his brother asked. At the reply of "yes," Frank looked at his brother aghast. "Then who did phone? Golly, this looks serious!"

Together the brothers raced outside the hotel to start their search.

"Dad's car certainly is gone," said Frank. "It was parked right over there."

"What's the matter? Lose something?" inquired a voice just then.

The boys looked around and noticed the proprietor of a store next to the hotel standing in front of his shop.

"Did you happen to notice anyone get into a car that was parked here a couple of hours ago?" Frank asked.

The man switched his cigar expertly from one side of his mouth to the other. "Sure did. Thought the owner was going to get a ticket for parking so close to that fire hydrant." The boys felt a qualm of conscience, for they had been guilty of this.

"Did you see him get into his car?" Joe pressed.

"There was a couple of fellows got into the car, near as I can remember," the shopkeeper stated.

"A *couple*—?" Joe stopped as Frank nudged him.

"Don't let this man know too much," the older boy whispered to his brother. "You can't tell who he is. Don't act so surprised." Aloud he continued, "Did you say two men?"

"Yes, it was two, all right. First there was a little fellow with a face like a doughnut. He got in the back seat. Then the other one came out. He was a big man. Good-looking. He got in front and drove off. But I didn't see the little man then."

"Thank you very much," said Frank breezily. He motioned to Joe and the two boys returned to the hotel lobby. "I suppose the fellow in the back was hiding when Dad came out," he observed gravely.

"Who do you suppose he was?" groaned his brother. "One of the trucking thieves, no doubt."

"I'm afraid so," agreed Frank. "And there's no telling where Dad is now. We don't know where to start investigating."

"I'll phone home," offered Joe. "Maybe Aunt Gertrude has a message for us. Dad might have some reason for not communicating with us here."

The lad stepped into a phone booth and called their number in Bayport. "Hello? Hello, Aunt Gertrude? Yes, this is Frank. Have you heard from Dad? No? What's that? The rehearsal?"

Though worried, the lad had to smile as he stepped outside.

"What's the joke?" asked Frank.

"Aunt Gertrude was all upset because we aren't there for a rehearsal of the play. She says Chet is mad as hops." Abruptly the boy's smile turned into a frown. "But she hasn't heard from Dad."

"Then we'll have to find him, and the sooner we get started the better," his brother said, his eyes blazing.

"You're right, Frank."

"There's no use trying to trail his car. That would be impossible. We haven't the slightest idea in which direction he went. There's only one thing I can think of for us to do right now.''

''Well, what is it?'' asked Joe.

''Watch all the wharves and freight stations. In that way we may see Moe Gordon driving a truck. Then we'll just have to trail him until we locate the place where his gang may be hiding Dad.''

''That's a big order,'' declared Joe. ''We've been trying to locate them all along.''

''We'll have to do it faster, that's all there is to it. We've a pretty good idea that the crooks kidnaped Dad. If they did, they probably took him to their headquarters.''

''Let's start at the nearest wharf and see if by chance any freight boats are putting in.''

The boys' task was a discouraging one. The first dock they approached was empty, and so was the second. As they neared the third, however, luck was with them.

''There's a freighter!'' cried Joe. ''Just sliding into her berth!''

''So it is,'' replied Frank. He parked their car and they jumped out. ''Keep your eyes open for suspicious-looking trucks.''

''There are a lot of vans over by that warehouse. Here's a 'Keep Out' sign,'' grinned Joe.

Despite it, the boys advanced along the edge of the wharf and watched the ponderous movement of the big vessel. At the same time a long line of trucks backed up to the waterfront. Suddenly Joe felt a rough hand grasp him by the collar and turn him around.

"Just what do you think you're doin'? We don't want any spies on this wharf," growled a gruff-looking police officer. "Waitin' for a chance to start trouble, are ye? Didn't ye see the sign?"

"Please, Officer—" appealed Frank.

"I been told to watch for a couple o' innocent-looking young fellows like you. Come along," the policeman commanded.

Despite their protests he took them to the station house, where Frank spoke to the desk sergeant.

"We aren't spies, Sergeant. We were just watching the ship come in."

The officer looked at the boy and his brother for several seconds. At length he leaned back, folding his arms behind his head.

"McNally, I think you've arrested the wrong fellows," he declared to the policeman. "But let me tell you this, boys. Don't hang around docks. We're trying to round up spies and you might be mistaken again for such people."

Thanking the officer, Frank and Joe hurried outside.

"If we can't even watch a ship coming into port, how are we ever going to find Gordon's gang and trace Dad?" the latter muttered in disgust.

"We'll just have to be more careful, that's all. I'm afraid, though, that it's going to be pretty tiresome and most discouraging waiting around for Gordon to put in an appearance.''

"Let's pay a call on Mr. Barker,'' suggested Joe.

"Instead of looking for Dad?''

"We'll never find Dad until we have more information than we have now. Perhaps if we find out what happened to Mr. Barker that night we'll have more to work on.''

Frank nodded thoughtfully. "I think you're right, Joe. Well, let's go.''

Turning toward the residential section of Aberdeen, they soon found themselves before the spacious lawns surrounding the man's estate. Frank shut off the motor after they had gone up the long, winding driveway.

"Mr. Barker is in, but I'm not sure he can see you,'' chanted a butler. "Just a minute.''

A moment later he returned, saying Mr. Barker would see them in the library. The Liberty Company president, looking somewhat pale and weak, greeted them cordially.

"Sit down, boys. I'm shocked over the disappearance of your father. Tell me, have you found any trace of him?''

Frank shook his head sadly. "We only know that when Dad started over to see you someone entered his car before he did.''

"Presumably your father was forced to drive somewhere at the point of a gun. You have informed the police?'' he queried.

"No, sir,'' said Joe. "Dad wouldn't want

us to, because then we'd have to divulge a lot of information about the trucking thieves that he doesn't want known yet.''

"We thought you might tell us what happened to you the night you were taken to the hospital, Mr. Barker," Frank suggested.

The executive's face looked grim. "Unfortunately, I can tell you very little. I was sitting in my office waiting for Hinchman. Being a little afraid he might try to do me physical harm, I looked about for something with which to defend myself."

"The sword?" Joe burst out.

The man gazed at the lad in mild surprise. "Why yes, I thought the Crusader's sword hanging above my desk might serve as a weapon, should I need one. I removed it from its sheath and placed it on a little table. Then I noticed some money lying on Miss Weed's desk." He paused, and sipped some water from a tumbler. He looked very pale.

"Perhaps we had better leave," suggested Frank.

"I am still somewhat weak from the ordeal," Mr. Barker smiled gravely, "but I want you to hear this. I decided to put the money in the safe. Just as I started to open it, all the lights went out."

CHAPTER XII

THE boys sat on the edge of their chairs, their eyes glowing in excitement. Mr. Barker drew out a large handkerchief and wiped his perspiring brow.

"At that instant I recall falling backward and hitting my head against something hard and sharp," the man said. "Next thing I knew I was in a hospital."

The ticking of the library clock punctuated the silence that followed.

"You were not attacked, Mr. Barker?" Joe queried. "Nobody hit you? You injured yourself by falling?"

The man shrugged. "They tell me at the hospital that I suffered a heart attack. Apparently no wound was inflicted on me except a scalp laceration caused by my fall. I'm completely mystified by the whole thing, boys."

Frank frowned. "But the money was stolen and the safe was rifled. You say you did not open the safe? Then somebody was in the room with you, Mr. Barker."

"The blade of the sword was broken off by the person trying to open the safe!" exclaimed Joe.

"And that is missing!" added Frank. "That's our clue to the intruder."

Mr. Barker was amazed to hear this but could offer no explanation.

"What was the name on the blade?" asked Frank eagerly.

"Edouard Poincelot."

"We've been wanting to find that out," said Joe. "It will help in our search."

The boys went on to tell Mr. Barker about their clue to the stolen estoque. He praised their efforts, and expressed the hope that the person who had taken the blade of the Crusader's sword would be apprehended soon.

"My main concern just now is about your father, however," he concluded.

"It is ours, too," said Joe, "but we don't know just what to do at the moment."

Frank had been quiet for several minutes. His eyes glistened as he leaned toward his host. "Will you do us a favor, Mr. Barker?" he asked excitedly.

"Certainly," replied the man, startled. "Anything within my power is yours for the asking."

"Will you lend Joe and me one of your trucks, Mr. Barker?"

The executive glanced at Frank in surprise. "W-why, of course, if you want it. I must confess that your request is a bit extraordinary. You understand how to operate big trucks?"

"Yes, and I have good reason for wanting it, sir. I promise you that we shall take good care of your property and pay for any damages."

Barker waved his hand. "Don't worry about that, boys. If you want one you may have it." He turned to a memorandum pad on his desk and scribbled a note. "Here is an authorization. Give this to Mr. Wagner at the factory and he'll see that you are taken care of."

Thanking the executive, the brothers hurried outside to their car. Joe's face bore a puzzled expression, so Frank at once explained his plan.

"It may not work at all, but I think it's worth the chance," he said. "We'll wear our overalls again and drive the truck to various garages. In that way we may find a trace of Gordon or the other thieves. The mechanics will be more apt to give us information if we're disguised as drivers."

"But—what garages, Frank? That's almost as bad as waiting around at all the wharves and freight stations."

"I think not, Joe. After all, those thieves have to stop for gas and repairs. Some of the garage attendants right around Aberdeen must know them. It's worth a try, anyhow."

At the Liberty Company they presented the note from Mr. Barker. Presently they were driving toward the hotel to change their clothes. The huge van was filled with empty boxes.

"Better park on a side street, Frank," suggested Joe. "If anybody's watching the hotel entrance, he'll be mighty suspicious of our actions."

Fifteen minutes later two truck drivers emerged from a side door of the Lenox Hotel and entered a Liberty Company truck at the curb not far distant.

"Let's take the highway from Aberdeen to Carside and stop at all the main garages on some pretext or other," suggested the older of the two fellows as they clattered off.

"Suits me," replied the other. "We need gas. Look at the gauge. Nearly empty. That's luck. We'll buy a little at a time at each place we come to."

The truck rumbled to a filling station a few minutes after leaving town.

"Five gallons, please," called out Frank as the attendant appeared. "Pretty warm day, ain't it?"

"Sure is," agreed the attendant. "You fellows drivin' trucks have a tough job, starin' at the road in the sun all day long."

"I'll say," said Frank. "And we got a long way to go, too."

"Goin' to Carside? Most of the fellers do that pass this way."

"I s'pose a lot of 'em stop here for gas, don't they?" Frank queried casually.

The attendant smiled broadly. "Man, this is the most popular station on this highway.

We get trucks from all over. Your company's
—you're a new driver for 'em, ain't you—and
the Williams Produce Company, Jones Moving
Van Company and a hundred others. Got a
new one about an hour ago. Klondike Company. Didn't like the fellow on it.''

Frank raised his eyebrows. ''You didn't like
him?''

''Naw. Most of you truck drivers are swell
guys. But the gink drivin' that Klondike bus
was a pain in the neck. Shriveled up little
shrimp, ugly as blazes, with a scar runnin'
across his cheek. And he has the nerve to get
tough with me.'' The man scowled.

''What was wrong with him?'' Joe asked.

''Just because I was busy with another customer and had to make him wait two extra
minutes for his gas he starts to holler at me.
I should o' smacked him one. Besides, there
was somethin' fishy about him.''

The boys were beside themselves with excitement. Only with great effort could Frank keep
his voice calm.

''Something fishy about him?'' he queried.

''Yeah. I heard some funny noises from inside his truck while I was fillin' 'er up. Sounded
like somebody with a gag in his mouth tryin' to
yell. The feller told me it was pigs. Said he
had a crate of 'em, but he didn't show 'em to
me. I dunno. It was mighty queer.''

This time Frank made no effort to hide his

excitement. "Which way did he go? Toward Carside? Put in ten more gallons." Two minutes later he added, "Here's your money. So long!"

Leaving the astonished attendant staring after them, the boys roared down the highway, their faces set and grim.

"Joe, I hope we're on the trail for certain this time!" cried Frank above the noise of the engine.

Traffic on the highway was heavy, and several hours elapsed before the boys reached the city of Carside. At once they began going up one street and down another to hunt for the truck marked Klondike Company.

It was a discouraging task. Many vans passed them, but none proved to be the one they were looking for. Then suddenly Joe spotted it near a large red brick building.

Frank decided to park their truck a block away from the spot. "We'd better do a little reconnoitering before we drive any farther," he told his brother.

"Right. That looks like a warehouse office there. Let's see who's in it," suggested Joe.

Casually the brothers strolled along the street until they were abreast of a large window on which was printed the name Great States Storage Company.

"We'd better not stop," whispered Frank. "Just glance in as we walk past."

The boys instinctively clutched each other at what they saw as they ambled by.

"Hinchman!" Joe exclaimed under his breath. "Wow, that's luck for us!"

"If this isn't being hot on the trail I don't know what is!" exulted Frank. "You remember he told Dad he had a moving business in Carside."

"We must get into that building without being recognized. Question is, how?" responded his brother softly.

"Look, Joe! There is another Klondike Company van parked in the alley. That gives me an idea." Frank stole over, examined the truck carefully, then became excited. "Look!" he whispered. "The name isn't painted on; it's only on a board that's screwed to the side. Let's put the sign on our truck over the Liberty name and then drive in!"

"And unload those empty boxes we're carrying? It's a long shot but it might work if we're not asked too many questions," said Joe.

Carefully the boys surveyed the scene and formed their daring plan. Fortunately the alley seemed to be deserted. They decided to drive the Liberty vehicle as close to the other as possible and then make a swift transfer of the sign. Rummaging around in the tool box, Joe drew forth a screw driver while Frank stood on guard.

"Nobody in sight," he reported.

"Keep watching. I'll have this thing off in half a minute."

There was a grinding sound as the lad pried loose the sign. "There it is, Frank. Just a second till I get the one on the other side."

"Hurry up, Joe. Some men are coming down the walk."

A moment later his brother had both boards stowed safely in their truck. To their relief the passers-by paid no attention to them. After they had gone Joe attached the new name to the Liberty van.

"Ready?" asked Frank.

As Joe jumped aboard, he started the engine. Guiding the truck, he brought it to a stop at the entrance to the Great States Storage Company.

"If anybody's watching us from the windows, we're done for," said Joe, gazing around dubiously.

"We'll have to take that chance. It'll be worth it if we can find Dad," Frank added, turning in.

"Suppose they ask us for our consignment papers?" queried Joe, as a new fear came to his mind.

"We'll cross our bridges when we come to them. Well, here goes."

With hearts high the boys went along the concrete driveway and came to a stop before the loading platform. A huge door suddenly rolled open and a burly man emerged.

"Where shall we put 'em?" inquired Frank, making his voice sound as gruff as possible.

"Second aisle behind them other crates," growled the man. Suddenly he stared at Frank. "Say, where'd you come from?" he asked suspiciously.

CHAPTER XIII

THE DISGUISE

CHILLS raced along the spines of the Hardy boys. Were they to be caught so soon?

"Where's Charley? Did he get another job?" the man at the warehouse door asked.

Frank thought fast. "Guess he has," he said, forcing a heavy laugh.

"Confound that Klondike Company!" exploded the man. "When are they goin' to stop sendin' green drivers over here? Well, get busy."

The boys heaved sighs of relief. They were still safe! Together they began unloading the empty boxes from their truck. The burly man watched them a few moments, then disappeared. Frank nudged his brother.

"Keep carrying in the stuff, Joe, while I take a look around," he told him.

Wending his way through the gloomy, cluttered interior of the warehouse, Frank saw nothing of interest at first. Then his eye fell on a glass door thickly coated with dust.

"An elevator!" he said, stepping alongside and pressing the button.

There was a loud clatter, then a prolonged bur-r-r as the lift eased down from somewhere high above. Frank yanked open the door and stepped within.

"Hm. Four floors," he mused, inspecting a panel of buttons inside. "Well, I'll start at the second and work up."

He pressed the corresponding button and the automatic elevator slowly ascended in a series of squeaks and rumblings. At the second landing Frank stepped out.

Footsteps were approaching the elevator! The boy jumped back into the car and pressed the fourth floor button. He was just in the nick of time. As the car rose past the second floor level he saw two men signaling to him.

"Wow! That was a close one! They'll have to wait till I get off," he muttered in relief.

The car stopped at the fourth floor. Opening the door, Frank peered out, expecting at any moment to find himself in the clutches of some suspicious official. Instead, he saw nothing but stacks of crates and boxes in the vast, silent room.

"What's that?" he suddenly asked himself. "Sounds like something scratching."

Every sense alert, he crept between two rows of boxes. Just then there was a loud *snap* and a stab of pain shot through his foot.

"Ouch!" Frank's cry was automatic.

A second later he could have kicked himself for his lack of restraint. Gazing downward, he saw that his right shoe was caught in a powerful rat-trap. With a jerk he tore it free.

"Now what? I suppose my yell will bring everybody in the place here in the next two minutes," he thought gloomily.

Again he heard the scratching sound. It was coming from a large box near an open window.

"That's strange!" thought the boy excitedly.

As he was about to bound toward the case, there was a sudden clatter at one end of the room. Frank looked up with a start.

"Here comes someone," the boy groaned in dismay. "I'd better hide!"

He stepped behind a high stack of crates just in time, for in a moment three men marched down the very aisle where he had been standing.

"You're crazy, Storch, not goin' through Hardy's pockets before you brought him up," one of his companions snarled.

"Oh, shut up!" snapped the other. "What's the use o' goin' through his pockets? He's in the carton, ain't he? He can't get out till we let him out, can he?"

"How do you know he can't? Some o' these detectives are regular Houdinis. They can get out of anything."

"All right, look for yourself and *see* if he got out."

Frank's heart was thumping so hard he was afraid the men would hear it! At that instant there was a series of loud clangs.

"That's the bell!" shouted Storch.

With a rush of feet the group raced toward the elevator and disappeared as quickly as they had come. Frank gazed after them in bewilderment, then bounded to the box. Leaning close to the top he made a trumpet of his fist and whispered:

"Dad! It's Frank!"

For a long second silence prevailed. Then came the muffled response, "Hurry!"

The boy looked around for a tool. Spying an old metal file lying on the floor, he set to work on the carton. In half a minute Mr. Hardy was free.

"Thank heaven you came," gasped the detective weakly. "I was all but suffocated."

"We'd better not waste any time, Dad. They may come back any minute. Are you all right?" He gazed at his parent with mingled feelings of relief and apprehension.

"I—I'll be all right, Frank," returned his father, making an obvious effort to steady himself. "We must find a way out. The elevator, of course, won't do. How about a——"

Once again there came the significant clatter and rumble from the end of the room.

"They're coming back, Dad!" cried Frank in alarm. "Quick, get behind those boxes!"

The rumble grew louder. It would be only a matter of seconds until the elevator would reach their floor. Fenton Hardy was shaking his head.

"There's no use in hiding here, Frank. They'll search the place. Find the fire escape. There surely must be one."

Leaving his father, the boy raced through the

gathering gloom from one end of the room to the other. In a jiffy he was back.

"It's down there at the far end, Dad. I tried the door and it's unlocked. Quick!"

Supporting the detective as best he could, Frank hurried him along the murky aisle.

"We'll have to pass the elevator to get to the fire escape, Dad. Hurry!"

"We'll—m-make it, F-Frank!" gasped his weakened father.

It seemed an eternity before the Hardys had passed the danger zone and reached the fire escape exit. The rumble of the lift suddenly ceased. In a babble of gruff voices several men stepped out. Frank gripped his father's arm and the Hardys froze in their tracks.

"Where is he?" piped the familiar voice of Hinchman.

"Over there in that big crate, Charlie," snapped another. "Hank, where's the light? First thing you know we'll be steppin' in the rat-traps."

Frank's heart was in his throat as an overhead bulb was snapped on. But he sighed in relief as the men moved in the direction of the broken carton.

With scarcely a sound the Hardys slipped through the fire escape door. Gulping in the fresh air, they picked their way cautiously down the winding steps.

"Keep your eyes open, Frank. We still may be seen," murmured Mr. Hardy.

They gazed below them as they descended. Thus far the alleyway seemed to be deserted.

"Dad, let's change clothes," suggested Joe. "There'll be less chance that they'll recognize you if we do."

"Good idea. There's a dark doorway right over there. That'll serve the purpose."

Swiftly the two removed their outer garments and made the exchange. At that instant a huge dog bounded up to them and began barking ferociously. Frank's heart sank as he spied a heavy-set man running toward his father and himself.

"Pretend you're a cripple, Frank," Mr. Hardy whispered. "Leave the rest to me."

As the man approached the wildly barking dog, he halted. Just emerging from the doorway was a lame boy leaning on the arm of an elderly companion in overalls.

"What's goin' on here?" demanded the newcomer after he had regarded them momentarily. "Did the dog bite the young feller?"

The elderly man shook his head. "No spik English. Son, he lame. Want work."

The other made an unpleasant grimace. "Guess you ain't the fellers I'm lookin' for. Get along with you! We're not needin' hired help."

He glared after the two as they walked slowly down the street and disappeared around a corner. Seeing no one about, Frank uttered a cry of joy. "Golly, Dad, that was great acting!

You certainly took the part of a newly-arrived foreigner. Whew! When that man first came up I thought we were going to be caught for certain."

Fenton Hardy's face looked grim. "Where did you leave Joe? Didn't he come with you?"

"Yes, Dad. I left him at the loading platform."

Frank gazed toward the building. "Our truck is gone! Joe must have taken it."

"Then he probably is safe. Now, we—" The detective stopped and wavered slightly.

"Dad! Are you ill?" Frank reached out just in time to keep his father from collapsing on the pavement. "Golly, I'd almost forgotten that you've been suffocating in a box and haven't eaten——"

"I—I'll be all right. Come, we must walk as fast as possible. Gordon and Hinchman and the rest of them will be after us any minute now. I'll lean on you a little and we'll make better time."

For a quarter of an hour father and son proceeded as rapidly as Mr. Hardy's depleted strength would permit. At length they found themselves in a better section of town. With a choice of restaurants on the main street Frank chose a Spanish one called "El Matador."

"That sounds interesting," he said, wondering if by any chance a former matador might run the place. "Let's go in there and get some nourishment," he urged.

The boy and his father entered a large room whose walls were attractively decorated with silken scarfs and crossed swords. A man in costume was playing a guitar softly.

The place was well filled with diners, but there were a few vacant tables. The headwaiter quickly stepped up to the Hardys.

"I'm sorry, but we have no more tables," he snapped.

"There's a vacant one over in the corner," observed Frank.

"That is reserved. We have no unoccupied tables."

"Please, waiter, my father needs—" Frank began, when he was interrupted by a loud, raucous voice.

"Lookit that! Lookit that! Raa-a!"

Frank turned scarlet. Then he spied a beautiful parrot in a cage a few feet away. Mr. Hardy broke into a low laugh.

"Frank, we forgot about our clothes!" he whispered.

Instantly father and son found themselves the center of all eyes. Conversation in the room stopped as the fashionable diners stared at them.

"You'll have to leave," ordered the waiter indignantly. "If you wish to eat, there is a hamburger stand near the station."

At this moment the manager came forward. One look at the faces of the Hardys told him they were not undesirable clients. While he could not blame his headwaiter, he did not wish to offend these people, so he motioned to them to follow him.

"I shall be glad to let you use this little room," he smiled. "And I shall get food for you myself. What would you like?"

"Thank you," said Mr. Hardy, sinking wearily into a chair. "I believe some hot soup would taste good."

During the meal it became evident that the manager suspected that the Hardys were in disguise and he tried hard to find out who they were. The detective and his son gave the man no inkling of their identity, but turned the conversation to the subject of swords.

"Do you collect them?" asked Frank.

"I used to when I traveled," the man replied, "but now I do not bother."

"How did you happen to give your place the name 'El Matador?'" the boy inquired a little later. "Do you enjoy bullfights?"

"Very much. But now the men are not so good. The last real fighter I saw was Castillo, but he gave up the sport and came to this country."

This bit of information startled Frank. Recalling the words of the antique dealer, Mr. Panser, about the man who had said he might sell his estoque to a matador, the Hardy boy wondered if he had suddenly come upon a clue to the person who had Mr. Barker's estoque.

CHAPTER XIV

"WHERE is this Castillo now?" Frank asked the proprietor of El Matador, hanging eagerly on the answer.

"I don't know," was the disappointing reply. "Probably working at something that has nothing to do with bullfighting."

The Hardys had finished their meal. As the detective paid the bill, he again thanked the owner for permitting them to eat and laughingly suggested that he let them out a side door. On the street, their troubles began again.

"We'd better take a taxi and go to the station," suggested Mr. Hardy. "I'm sure Joe would be most apt to wait for us there. If he isn't there, we'll take a train to Aberdeen. I left some papers at the hotel I must pick up."

It was some time before they could find a taximan to take them. Two drivers looked at their clothes askance and would not stop. A third let them get in but insisted upon being paid his fare before moving!

"There'll be a train in twenty minutes," Frank told his father when they reached the station and spoke to the agent. "That'll give us time to——"

He stopped short as a familiar low whistle sounded almost at his elbow.

"Yes, it's I," grinned Joe, who seemed to have appeared from nowhere. "Hello, Dad, I'm certainly glad to see you. We'd better not stay around here. Follow me."

Pleased and relieved, Fenton Hardy walked rapidly after his two excited sons. Joe led the way to the rear of the depot, then halted and peered around furtively.

"We're not safe anywhere in this city," he whispered. "Gordon, Hinchman and the rest are after us, I'm certain of that. They think we know too much!"

"From their point of view, I guess we do," smiled the detective. "I wish we had more evidence. An arrest now wouldn't prove much."

"I've hidden our truck in a barn outside of town and taken off the Klondike signs. I think we ought to get out there right away. We'll have to take a taxi—" he looked at his father— "but we'd better be careful which one."

"Wait here and I'll get a cab," said Frank.

He slipped away and watched a line of cars alongside the station. Satisfied at last that no suspicious-looking characters were driving them he summoned one. In a jiffy he had signaled to Joe and Mr. Hardy and all three got in.

"Number 38 Grove Pike," ordered Joe in a low voice, and the cab chugged off.

Frank gazed at his brother expectantly. "What happened after I left you, Joe? Did they catch you with the boxes?"

The younger lad made a wry face. "Pretty

nearly, but not quite," he whispered. "I went on unloading them after you left. All of a sudden, just as I had finished, Hinchman came down to the platform. He didn't recognize me, but he wanted to know what our truck had brought."

Frank leaned toward his brother eagerly. "What did you do then?"

Joe chuckled. "I said I was just a hired driver and didn't know anything about what I had carried. He asked me a lot more questions and I pretended I didn't know anything. Then I suggested he go inside and take a look at the boxes himself."

"Did he?" Mr. Hardy queried.

"Yes. Then I thought I better skip! I jumped into the truck and got away as fast as I could."

"Good work," said the detective. "Another two minutes and you'd have been caught."

"Don't I know it? Well, I had a hunch that if Frank had found you, Dad, you probably would decide to take a train to Aberdeen. Anyhow, I took that chance and here we all are! Driver, here's the place," he said, and they drew up in front of a rambling farmhouse.

"Nobody lives here," Joe whispered as he led the others to the rear of the building and into the barn. "Here's the truck. Apparently it hasn't been touched. I piled hay in the back. Dad, you and Frank had better hide in it till we get to Aberdeen."

"Let's you and I change clothes first, Frank," suggested Mr. Hardy. "After all, I'm bigger than you, and these clothes of yours are pretty snug," he laughed.

The exchange was made. A few minutes later the huge truck was on the highway, humming along at a steady pace. Mr. Hardy and Frank, snugly ensconced in the pile of hay in the rear, talked over plans for their next move.

"I think I'll phone the Carside police and have them keep an eye on Hinchman's warehouse," said the detective. "They may be able to furnish us with valuable evidence."

Very weary from his recent experiences, Mr. Hardy presently fell asleep. The next thing he knew his younger son was opening the back door and saying:

"All out! Aberdeen! We're a block from the hotel. Better get out here and walk. I think we ought not to drive over to the entrance. Somebody may be watching."

"How about you going to the hotel, Dad?" suggested Frank, "and Joe and I returning Mr. Barker's truck?"

The plan was agreeable to the detective, so the boys set forth immediately. Leaving the vehicle at the Liberty Company, they took their car and stopped at the executive's residence.

"What, back so soon?" greeted the man affably from a wheel chair. "I thought you'd be gone for days. Tell me, have you heard anything from your——"

"We've found him, Mr. Barker, thanks to

you for lending us a truck," beamed Frank.

"You've found him? I'm glad! Come sit down and tell me about it."

The boys related their story and told of the suspicious activities of Hinchman. When they had finished, Mr. Barker promised them any further assistance he might be able to give.

"We have a clue to the identity of a matador named Castillo, now in this country," said Frank. "Putting two and two together, we think a matador may have your stolen estoque, so we're going to try to find this Castillo."

"Good," smiled Mr. Barker. "It seems to me you Hardys have several big tasks to accomplish."

"The hardest one to figure out is the broken sword in your office," said Joe. "Why didn't the intruder take the hilt? That is the valuable part."

"But the blade is the weapon," offered Mr. Barker. "Oh, I keep hoping that whoever has it isn't using it for some sinister purpose. I shiver every time I think it might have been used on me. Maybe it was fortunate I was unconscious when the thief came in."

"Have you another estoque anything like the one which was stolen?" asked Frank.

"No, I haven't," the man replied. "It is very rare. But I have a photograph of it. Let's go into the museum and I'll show it to you."

Joe wheeled the man in and the boys looked at a colored picture of a small, beautiful weapon, richly studded with jewels. The Hardys were not likely to mistake the original, should they find it.

"It's a coincidence that we have come across two mysteries about swords so recently," said Joe. "Just before leaving home my brother and I were practicing a fencing act for a show we are going to be in."

"Chet Morton, a friend of ours back home," Frank explained further, "is chairman of a play to be given for charity. In it Joe and I are supposed to fight a duel with swords."

"Up to the present we've used umbrellas for weapons," laughed Joe.

Without a word Mr. Barker smilingly reached up and unhooked two swords from the wall. "If these will be of any help to you in your play, I'll lend them to you gladly. Here you are," he offered with a smile.

"Oh, Mr. Barker, do you really mean it?" Joe gasped, his eyes shining.

Frank likewise was excited over the unexpected offer. "We'll be *very* careful of them, Mr. Barker," he promised.

"Be very careful not to kill each other with them," said the elderly man with a twinkle in his eyes. "The blades are sharp, as you will notice. I wish you all manner of success with your play!"

Thanking the gentleman, the boys departed, then headed for the Lenox Hotel.

"You know," said Frank when their elation over receiving the swords had abated somewhat, "I've a feeling we ought to check out of this hotel."

"If we go marching in there with these two weapons we'll probably be asked to check out!" laughed Joe.

"I hate to leave them in the car all night," said Frank.

"If Gordon or Hinchman should be spying on us at the Lenox, they would love to get their hands on them," added his brother.

"We might hide the swords under that blanket in the back there," suggested Frank, "and leave the car locked in a garage a few blocks away. We can walk from there."

This plan was carried out. Upon reaching the hotel, the boys went directly to their father's room. He was in bed but not asleep.

After hearing about the swords, he gasped and warned the boys to be mighty careful of them. They promised, then told him of their idea of checking out of the hotel in the morning.

"We'll do it," he agreed. "And now we all must get some sleep. But before you turn in, will you report to the police the theft of my car? When I was kidnaped, the thieves took it away. Good night, boys. And thanks again for my rescue," he smiled.

In the morning the two brothers got their automobile. They had just put their bags in the back of it, when their father came toward them with a stranger.

"This chap tells me he knows where my

stolen car is," he announced. "He suggests we follow him. His coupé is over there."

As the three Hardys trailed the man in the boys' car they discussed the probable truth of his statements.

"It may be a trick," muttered Frank.

"Well, we have two swords with us in case of trouble," Joe chuckled.

"We'll have to be wary," cautioned their father.

For some time the Hardys followed the man through outlying districts until they found themselves on a narrow road in a tangled wilderness.

"I can't say I like the looks of this place," said Joe apprehensively. "What's that fellow up to, anyhow?"

"We'll soon find out," observed Frank. "He's stopping. He's waving to us."

"He wants us to get out of the car and follow him on foot. Shall we go?"

"Certainly," broke in Mr. Hardy. "But watch out."

"Dad, the walking is dreadful," said Frank. "Won't you please wait in the car? But lock yourself in. We don't want you to disappear again!"

Mr. Hardy, feeling not too strong yet, agreed.

"Come on, Joe!" urged Frank.

The stranger was moving through the underbrush. With set lips and fists ready for action the boys followed him.

CHAPTER XV

"WE have a short walk ahead of us. I hope you won't mind it too much."

The bronzed young man had turned in his tracks and was waiting for Frank and Joe to come up to him.

"Your father's car is on the other side of the marsh near the shore," he continued as the boys approached him. "Just follow me."

For several moments the lads floundered about among water-soaked reeds, stumbling through boggy sand that came at times above their knees.

"This is a trap of some sort, you just wait and see," Joe declared under his breath. "We were fools to fall into it so easily."

The group plodded on. The stranger uttered not a word. Joe was growing more and more impatient. He hurried up behind the tanned young man.

"See here, I think we've gone far enough. Just where are you taking us?" he demanded.

The fellow shaded his eyes and squinted through some dense reeds. Then he turned to Joe with a broad smile. "See it?"

Skeptically the boy gazed ahead in the direction the stranger had indicated. Then he shouted, "Frank! There it is! That is Dad's car!"

"You see, I was telling you the truth," the young man said in a pleasant voice. "I chanced to see the automobile early this morning while I was fishing. I looked inside and saw the name Fenton Hardy on an envelope in the dashboard pocket. I telephoned your home and found out you were at the Lenox."

"That was mighty fine of you," said Joe, ashamed of his suspicions. His brother echoed his sentiments.

Frank was staring at the vehicle. "Golly, look at it. Must be down to the hubs in the sand. How do you suppose it ever got to this place?"

"Auto thieves sometimes get scared after they take a car," offered the fisherman, and the boys did not enlighten him on the real truth.

"I'll miss my guess if we don't have a bad time getting it out of those ruts," said Frank.

The Hardys inspected the mired vehicle, which appeared undamaged. Frank stepped on the starter and the engine roared into life, but the car failed to budge.

"We must have planks," suggested the stranger. "I believe I can get some from my boat at the beach."

The boys accompanied the obliging man a few dozen yards distant to a place where they came upon a dory on the sand.

"We'll take the thwarts out of her, fellows. And here's a rope. We ought to be able to get the car out if we put the boards under the wheels, tie the rope to the axle and pull."

The scheme worked admirably. Frank sat at the wheel and as soon as the car was on dry ground the other two jumped in. After a short, rough ride they turned into the lane where the waiting cars were parked. Fenton Hardy hailed them delightedly and chatted for several moments with the stranger, whose name was Henry Farnsworth.

"I really don't want a reward," he said as the detective pulled out a wallet. "I'm glad to have been of service to you—always wanted to meet you," he smiled.

"Well, Dad, how about getting started?" suggested Frank, when Mr. Farnsworth left.

He followed his father and brother in the salvaged car. He had gone barely half a mile when the engine sputtered and died. Again and again the boy pressed the starter but without result. Joe and Mr. Hardy turned about and came alongside in the other automobile.

"What's the matter?" called Joe.

"Probably sand in the motor. Guess we'll have to tow the old bus along," replied his brother, fumbling in the tool box for a stout rope.

They tied the rope to both cars. It was a slow, tedious ride, but at length they found a large repair shop on the outskirts of the city.

While a mechanic worked on the stalled engine, the boys and their father ambled about impatiently inside the garage. Suddenly Mr. Hardy motioned to his sons.

"Did you notice the truck that just drove up to that gasoline pump?"

Outside could be seen a large, dust-covered van. The driver was ordering the attendant to hurry.

"Just an ordinary truck, so far as I can see," observed Joe, scrutinizing the scene. "Can't say I like the looks of the driver, though."

"That is exactly what I was thinking," murmured Mr. Hardy. "Frank, see if you can find out anything about him without too much fuss."

The boy strolled outside. As Joe and his father watched, they could see Frank casually talking first with the driver, then with the attendant. As the truck departed, Frank hurried back to his companions.

"He's picking up a shipment at the main wharf in Aberdeen," he whispered. "That's all I could find out. He wasn't a very pleasant fellow."

"Do you think we'd better follow him, Dad?" Joe queried tensely.

The detective's eyes narrowed. "Boys, I may be wrong, but I have a hunch that driver is one of the thieves. Better check on him to make certain. I'll wait here until my car is fixed."

His sons needed no second bidding. The man

had not gone far before they were out on the highway.

"What company is he representing?" Joe asked his brother as they sped along. "I didn't see his sign."

"The Noonian Oriental Rug Company, I think it was. Golly, look at him speed!"

"Better not get too close to him. He might get suspicious."

"We'll have to take that chance. I don't want to lose him in this traffic. There he is! He's turning off," said Frank.

"That's the road leading to the wharf," announced Joe. "Maybe we'd better park soon and walk the rest of the way."

"This will do," said Frank presently. "We'll get out here."

"There's a vessel unloading," cried Joe. "And there goes the truck alongside. Incidentally, we'd better watch out for wharf policemen. They don't seem to like us."

With every sense alert, the boys hurried between rows of sheds near the dock until they came to the long platform beside which a freight vessel was moored. Not far from it stood the big truck.

"Where's the driver?" Frank wondered.

"There he is," replied Joe. "Showing his bills of lading to one of the ship's officers."

Two figures could be seen standing not far distant, one in rough garments, the other in trim maritime attire. At length the men separated. Simultaneously a large door opened in the side of the ship, disclosing stacks of crates.

"Here comes the cargo, Frank!"

Several burly men, the truck driver among them, began transferring the boxes from the ship to the van.

"Well," said Joe with a show of impatience, "what are we going to do about it?"

"We haven't proved there's anything wrong yet, but I know a way to find out. We'll phone the Noonian Oriental Rug Company."

"Great idea, Frank! I'll do it. You wait here and watch."

His brother slipped away. For some time Frank watched the unloading process. Bit by bit the height of the piled cases increased. It was evident that the task was nearly complete.

"What on earth is keeping Joe?" the older boy mused with growing apprehension.

Several of the workmen disappeared, their services no longer necessary. By craning his neck Frank could see that only a few crates still remained in the vessel's hold. His heart sank at the thought that the truck might get away. Then Joe returned.

"Dad was right!" he said. "That van belongs to the thieves! The cargo's being stolen! And it's a very valuable one, too."

Frank's firm jaw dropped. "Really?" He grabbed his brother by the sleeve. "Come on, we must do something. We'll get the po——''

"I've already called the police. They're on their way. Should be here in five minutes.''

"They'd better hurry. Look, the unloading is just about finished.''

In an agony of suspense the boys watched the last box being carried to the truck. The door in the vessel's side slammed shut. The heavy-set figure disappeared, and they could hear the cough of the powerful engine.

"Sirens! The police! Boy, they're getting here just in the nick of time!'' cried Joe happily.

The wail grew louder and louder, drowning the sound of the truck's motor. The vehicle was backing around to head out from the wharf. An instant later three official cars roared up.

"Stop!'' came a chorus of shouts, and a group of officers rushed up to the driver.

In a second Frank and Joe had joined them.

"One of you the fellow who called us?'' demanded a policeman, spying the Hardys. "Come along with us to the station. Fred! Jim! Take that truck driver in the patrol wagon.''

A quarter of an hour later the group stood in front of the sergeant's desk. Joe told him the whole story. Sullenly the captive glared at the circle of faces around him but refused to answer the questions put to him.

"All right, you stay here till you loosen that tongue of yours,'' snapped the sergeant at length. He turned toward the boys. "Many thanks, fellows. We may need you later, but you can go now."

Once outside, the lads hesitated. "Where do you suppose we'll ever find Dad, Frank?" speculated his brother.

"Let's call the garage. There's a chance he may be there still."

Fenton Hardy was located at the place. He was astounded and delighted at the news.

"Stay where you are, Frank. I'll be right over," he said.

When he arrived, his sons related the details of what had happened.

"Good work!" applauded their father. Then his face grew grim. "We've another task ahead of us. I've just talked to headquarters at Carside. We're to go there right away. They have some evidence against Hinchman."

Without further ado the three departed, Frank and Joe following their father in their own car. As the lights of Carside loomed ahead of them, a street under repair made it necessary for them to make a detour.

"Isn't that Hinchman's warehouse over there?" asked Joe a few minutes later. "Sure it is. Gee, Frank, look out!"

A car which had shot from an alleyway alongside the building was now racing toward them at terrific speed. It nearly hit the Hardy car, then swerved around the corner, its tires whining.

"Well, I'll be—" exploded Joe, shaking his fist at the departing vehicle.

"Perhaps we'd better chase that fellow," said Frank. "He may be somebody we're after."

Twisting the wheel around, he tore after the retreating car, which turned first one corner, then another. When the boys veered into the main road they saw no sign of the vehicle they were pursuing.

"Oh, well," Joe sighed, "let's go back and find Dad."

As they came near the warehouse again, Frank slowed down to look at the huge structure of the Great States Storage Company. At the same instant came the sound of a terrific explosion.

CHAPTER XVI

"FRANK! Hinchman's building has been blown up. It's falling!"

"Golly, the whole thing's caving in!" Joe gasped. "How do you suppose it happened?"

"Wonder if anybody was hurt. Let's investigate," Frank suggested as a shower of plaster dust arose above the tumbling bricks. "It might be a good time to look at the company's records, too. Let's see if we can find any of them. They'd be valuable evidence."

Tensely the brothers waited until the toppled structure had settled. Then, coughing and sneezing, they hurried through the haze that hung over the street. Finally they approached the spot where the entrance to the warehouse had been.

"The office was about there, Frank, under that pile of wreckage."

"Question is, how are we going to get to it? Let's see if we can find an opening. Maybe the room isn't entirely ruined."

The boys crawled up on top of the debris and peered through the chinks and cracks.

"Ouch!"

Joe clapped a hand to one shoulder. He

gazed upward ruefully. "A brick, Frank. Golly, I'd almost forgotten that parts of the walls are still standing. Better watch out."

The words were scarcely out of his mouth when there was a loud rat-tat-tat and a hail of loose plaster cascaded over them. The boys ducked.

"Oh, for a helmet," the younger lad wailed after the sound had subsided.

"I could use a whole suit of armor," laughed his brother.

"Say, hand me your flashlight a minute." Frank poked the instrument through a large crevice in the pile of debris. "It's the office, Joe! Hardly scratched! Look!"

Intently they gazed at the fairly intact room beneath the wreckage. Frank swung the light to and fro. "There's the office safe, Joe!"

"Yes, and look at it. The door's ajar."

"I suppose the explosion or whatever it was blew it open. Stay here and hold the light. I'm going down to get a closer view."

Joe played the light over the room as his brother climbed gingerly through the loose boards and plaster. He began poking about. Presently he stepped into the open again, his face registering keen disappointment.

"The safe's empty," Frank announced. "So are the desk drawers. There's nothing down there except that stack of boxes you can see in the corner."

"Hmph. What's in them?"

"Looked like a lot of junk to me. Old tools, saws, files, some coils of wire. Nothing very valuable."

For several moments neither of the boys spoke as they watched a fast gathering crowd of people. Then Joe cried out, "Why didn't I think of that before?"

"Think of what?"

"Remember the speeding car we chased?"

"I'll say I do."

"I'll bet Hinchman and his cronies were in it, making a quick getaway with all their records and valuables."

Frank Hardy knit his brow thoughtfully. Then he nodded.

"It's perfectly possible. They decided the trail was too hot, so they set a time bomb to destroy whatever evidence they couldn't carry with them."

"Exactly, Frank. Come on, let's find Dad. He's probably at the police station."

The wail of sirens interrupted them, and a moment later several police cars came to a stop. Shouts filled the air.

"There's Dad!" Joe exclaimed, spying the familiar figure of their father accompanying the officers.

The boys hurried over to the detective, who greeted them with a frown. "Boys, it looks as if they've outsmarted us. I was hoping we could snare the gang before they might guess what we were up to."

The Hardys drew aside and watched the eerie play of lights and the scrambling figures of the policemen. The boys related how they had investigated the buried office, but had found nothing of importance.

"I'm not surprised at that," muttered their father. "And that's not the worst of it, either. I went to the police station expecting some news after their message and found that they merely wanted to ask me a few more questions about Hinchman."

"Do you mean that the authorities haven't discovered a single thing after all their watching, Dad?" Frank queried, unbelieving.

Mr. Hardy shook his head in disgust. "Not an iota, although they say they've had a special man watch the warehouse day and night for a week." The detective's voice sank to a whisper. "I've a feeling that someone on the police force is in cahoots with Hinchman, boys."

"I wonder if they moved out all the stuff," said Joe. "If so, it will be pretty conclusive proof that they blew up the place on purpose. Let's see what we can find out."

Again the boys scrambled about the wreckage after obtaining police permission to do so. Although they searched as thoroughly as possible in the ruins, they could find no remnants of crates, boxes or any of the contents the cartons might have held.

"The next thing to do is to inquire of people working in the vicinity whether they noticed a lot of stuff being moved out within the past day or so," said Frank.

Between them the brothers interviewed a superintendent of a brick yard, the proprietor of a quick lunch stand, and several other persons. No one had noticed any particularly heavy movement of trucks.

"Guess we're licked," decided the older boy at last, hot and weary.

Joe, not as apt to become discouraged as Frank, said suddenly, "The stuff had to be taken away somehow. There's a river down there. Maybe a boat was loaded with Hinchman's stolen stuff."

"But somebody would have seen it being taken out," objected Frank.

"Not if it was carried away underground."

"Underground! You mean a tunnel?" asked Frank excitedly.

"Exactly," replied Joe. "It may be a wild guess, but I'd like to do some hunting."

"One thing's certain," said Frank. "We can't look under the debris for an entrance to a tunnel. We'll have to look down by the river for the exit."

Drawing an imaginary line from the wrecked warehouse to the river, the brothers hastened with all possible speed toward the water. It was a moonless night, so both boys made sure they had their flashlights.

Carefully they picked their way down the embankment, then the brothers separated, one going right, the other left of the spot they had picked. In a few minutes Frank's light showed up a large door in the side of the cliff. He whistled softly for his brother.

"I think we ought to look there," he said when Joe reached him.

He pointed his light. At the same time the heavy door swung outward and a furtive face appeared. At once it disappeared again.

"Let's get closer," whispered Frank.

Cautiously the two boys reached the spot and climbed to the ground above the door. Again it opened.

"I guess it's all right now," said a voice. "Got that record book of Hinchman's?"

"Yes," replied another man. "We'll make a dash for it and join him before the police get us."

Together the two started down the embankment. At the same instant the boys jumped from their perch.

"I'll take the one ahead!" cried Frank, racing after the figure that in fright had leaped forward.

The fellow behind him suddenly threw up his arms. A dark object sailed through the air and landed with a dull *plop* at the water line.

"The book of records!" groaned Joe as he tackled the man.

Young Hardy was no match for the steel muscles against which he grappled. He would have lost his man entirely had not his brother returned to help him. The fellow Frank had chased evidently was very familiar with his surroundings and had disappeared in the darkness.

"Let go of me!" demanded their captive, struggling to free himself. "You got no right to do this. I'll call the police."

"That's exactly what we're going to do," Frank said grimly.

The man protested at each step, so that the Hardys were panting vigorously by the time they reached the top of the embankment. To their relief a patrolman was standing on the next corner. He summoned a car, which quickly carried the group to headquarters. As they entered the desk sergeant uttered a cry.

"Jackson! What's the meaning of this?"

A policeman standing near the boys whispered, "You've nabbed one of our special detectives, fellows! What's he been up to?"

The boys, turning to the officer, told their story. Following it the detective, facing a circle of grim policemen, was forced to speak up.

"I don't know anything, honest I don't," he whined. "All I know is the warehouse gang has been takin' stuff in boxes out of the tunnel and puttin' it on boats."

"Where did they take it?" demanded the sergeant.

The prisoner shrugged. "I don't know. I didn't help 'em. I just watched 'em. I didn't do anything wrong, honest!"

"Who was the man with you tonight?" asked Frank. "The one who got away."

"The head bookkeeper," growled Jackson.

The sergeant nodded toward Frank and Joe. "Thanks, fellows, for catching this culprit for us. We've been suspecting for some time there was funny work going on. You can go now, though we'll probably need you later. Good night."

Dawn had hardly brightened the eastern sky when Frank and Joe were stumbling through the ruins of the warehouse again. After they had slipped and slid for two hours their search still had revealed nothing. They had just decided to go off for some breakfast, when Joe's foot suddenly kicked something sharp beneath a chunk of plaster. He bent low and picked it up.

"Look at this!" he cried. "It's part of a sword blade!" In his hand he held a piece of metal about four inches long. Turning it over, he saw engraved the letters "CELOT." "What was the name on the Crusader's sword?" he added excitedly.

"Edouard Poincelot," replied Frank.

"Then here is a piece of Mr. Barker's broken sword!" exclaimed his brother.

Thrilled, Frank examined the fragment of steel. "It's part of the missing blade, sure as you're alive!" he agreed. "That definitely links Hinchman and his pals with the theft and accident in Mr. Barker's office."

"I wonder where the rest of the blade is," said Joe. "Let's look for it."

Eagerly the brothers renewed their search, but no other piece of the metal came to light. At last they decided to give up the hunt.

"No doubt the person who was holding the blade when this piece we've just found snapped off still has it," said Frank.

"Let's hope so," added Joe. "I'd like to return every part of Edouard Poincelot's sword to Mr. Barker."

"And catch the thief on two counts," said Frank. "Well, let's get started. Where do you suggest we begin?"

"Down by the river," replied Joe grimly.

CHAPTER XVII

At Joe's suggestion the Hardy boys decided to look along the water for the book of records tossed away by the stranger coming from the tunnel the night before.

"Suppose you fish around in the water," said Joe, "while I investigate the tunnel. May find something interesting there."

Frank fumbled in the muddy water for a while without success. Discouraged, he ambled downstream, gazing about him idly. Suddenly he stopped, peered ahead into a clump of reeds at the water's edge, then waded out to a drifting rowboat.

"If that book on the back seat is the one we want, then we're in luck," the boy said to himself excitedly.

Reaching the moving craft, he picked up the large, black-covered volume. It was marked "Ledger." Frank shouted for his brother as he splashed back to dry ground.

"What's up?" cried Joe, joining him.

"I've found the book of records of the Great States Storage Company," his brother cried. "Some evidence!"

"Hurrah!" said Joe, thumping the other on the back. "Let me see it."

Quickly the two thumbed through the volume, growing more excited with each revealing page. It was clear that they now possessed evidence which would insure the conviction of the trucking thieves.

"But we still haven't caught the crooks," Frank remarked with a dry chuckle. "What good is the evidence without the men responsible for it?"

"Not much, I guess," his brother admitted. "Well, let's get back to the hotel and tell Dad what we've found."

Mr. Hardy suggested that he and his sons return to Bayport to study the contents of the ledger and formulate fresh plans for trapping the lawless men. As they drove up to the Hardy house on Elm Street some time later, the boys' chum Chet Morton rushed out to greet them.

"It's about time you fellows came back," he snorted in mock rage. "I was just asking your Aunt Gertrude where you were. How do you suppose I can manage a play if half the actors are missing?"

Frank winked at his brother. "We've been getting some stage props, Chet," he grinned, reaching under the car seat and bringing forth the two swords Mr. Barker had lent him and his brother.

The stout boy gulped. "G-good night, where'd you get those wicked-looking things?"

"We'll tell you all about them later, Chet,"

Joe smiled. "In the meantime, how about a rehearsal?"

"We're having one this evening. That's what I came over for. Your aunt invited me to dinner. We'll go right afterward."

Promising their father that they would be home early, the brothers set out for the high school auditorium with their stout chum. As they drove along they related some of their experiences, telling of the stolen estoque which they thought might be in the hands of a matador named Castillo, and also about the Crusader's sword. The stout boy listened wide-eyed. When Frank mentioned the broken blade, Chet's jaw dropped another inch.

"Do you m-mean to say that those things can snap off?" he stammered, leaning away from the weapons Joe was holding.

"Well, the one that was hanging in Mr. Barker's office did, but these two are all right —so far," said the Hardy lad in mock gravity. "Of course, you never can tell what will happen when we start dueling."

Chet gazed at the weapons fearfully. "Well, all I can say is I'm glad *I'm* not doing the dueling. That'll be your worry."

Still teasing their fat chum, the brothers reached the auditorium where presently they joined the other players. The group already was rehearsing. Chet's sister Iola and her pretty friend Callie Shaw shrieked when Frank and Joe began brandishing their swords.

"On guard!" exclaimed Joe, making a thrust at his brother.

"On guard yourself!" retorted Frank with a parry.

There was a series of loud clanks as the swords clashed. The boys soon found themselves surrounded by the other members of the cast.

"Stab him, Joe! Attaboy!"

"Look out, Frank! Now's your chance!"

The clank of metal mingled with the shouts and cheers of the onlookers. Grunting and panting, the Hardys chased each other all over the platform. Suddenly someone yelled:

"Look out! The scenery's falling!"

The milling group scattered, and not a second too soon. Only a plump, slow-moving figure was left in the center of the stage.

"Ouch! I'm killed!" cried Chet a second later.

Convulsed with laughter, Frank and Joe went to their chum's assistance, pulling aside a "garden wall" which had dropped from its ropes overhead.

"You're not killed—quite," said Joe.

The fat boy surveyed himself ruefully. "It's all your fault," he grumbled, looking at Frank and Joe accusingly. "If you hadn't made so much rumpus with those confounded swords, you wouldn't have shaken the scenery loose!"

"Never mind, I guess it can be fixed," said

Frank, making an effort to keep his face straight. "Come on, let's all get to work."

With the help of the others in the group, they soon had the "garden wall" restored to its proper place. Chet's expression gradually brightened.

"That'll be all right, I guess," he announced. "Well, enough rehearsing for tonight, everybody. See you all tomorrow."

As the group broke up, Frank and Joe sought out Callie and Iola.

"Oh, I suppose we might let you two musketeers take us home," giggled Callie. "That is, if you'll promise not to play any tricks with those horrible swords."

The boys promised, and as soon as Chet joined them they went to Bayport's leading confectionery for a midnight snack. After a round of sodas and much hilarity Frank and Joe drove Chet and the girls to their homes, then headed toward their own.

"I hope Dad won't be angry with us. We said we'd be home early to study that ledger with him," Frank reminded his brother as they turned into Elm Street.

"I think he won't mind. We'll look it over first thing in the——"

Frank glanced suddenly at his brother. "What's the matter, Joe?"

"Slow down. I thought I saw somebody on our lawn."

The Hardy home loomed up in the darkness ahead. Frank quickly stopped the engine and switched off the headlights.

"I don't see anybody, Joe."

"Sh. Look by the hedge."

"Oh! I see him! He's crouching there. He must be waiting for us. Let's scare him."

With bated breaths they watched the motionless figure. Then, taking care not to make a sound, Joe reached beneath the car seat and drew out the swords. He handed one to Frank. Without a word the boys crept from the automobile and approached the hedge. Then, on a single impulse, they rushed toward the spot.

"Get out of there!" Joe yelled, with weapon outstretched.

There was a loud rustle near the bushes and a dark figure flitted into the gloom.

"He went that way," Frank whispered.

Together the Hardys tore over the broad lawn, but the intruder was nowhere to be seen. After a careful search of the premises the boys gave up.

"Just an old tramp, I suppose," observed Frank. "Come on, let's go in and get some sleep."

To their surprise, Mr. Hardy was standing on the staircase in his pajamas, frowning. "What's all the yelling about, boys?" he asked.

When Joe related what had happened the detective's scowl deepened. "For goodness' sake, you've been chasing Smalley, the private detective I engaged to watch our property. Some sleuths my sons are turning out to be!''

The brothers looked at each other sheepishly. ''We're sorry, Dad. We didn't know——''

''Never mind. Hurry to bed. I'll have to go out and find the poor fellow.''

As their parent threw on a coat and disappeared outside Frank and Joe started upstairs. The latter halted midway and held up his forefinger.

''Frank! Did you hear that?''

A sound like the soft swish of stealthy footsteps could be heard overheard. Mystified, the boys stared wide-eyed. Somewhere a board squeaked loudly.

''Shall we switch on the lights upstairs?'' Joe whispered.

The other boy shook his head. ''We'd better investigate first.''

Joe thrust out his sword and began advancing noiselessly up the long staircase, with Frank close behind. At the top landing the former halted again and for a long moment the boys listened. The footsteps sounded once more, this time close at hand. Joe pointed his sword into the darkness of the hall. Then came an unearthly shriek that froze the boys in their tracks.

''Ouch! Oh, I've been murdered!''

Frank fumbled for the light switch and snapped it on. To the brothers' amazement Aunt Gertrude lay on the floor, moaning.

"My goodness, is she hurt?" Frank exclaimed, as he bent to examine her.

"Is that you, Frank Hardy?" demanded the woman, suddenly sitting bolt upright. Seeing their swords she shrieked again. "I knew it, oh, I knew it! I knew I should be murdered by one of those terrible weapons! Aren't you boys ashamed of yourselves?"

"Are you h—hurt, Aunt Gertrude?" stammered Joe.

"Am I hurt? Of course I'm hurt! Just look at this kimono! Look at this horrible rip!"

Seeing that their aunt, despite the tear in her gown, had not been scratched in the slightest, the boys heaved sighs of relief. Joe, in fact, found it hard to suppress his laughter as the irate woman continued her tirade against them.

"Just you wait till I tell your father of this. Imagine! Running through a dark house with swords! Why, I—I cannot understand why I am still alive!"

"But you *are* alive, Aunt Gertrude," Joe ventured.

"Never mind, I might not have been," snapped his relative. With a final glare of disapproval in their direction she turned and flounced back to her bedroom.

"Well, that's that," said Frank. "And a narrow escape, too. Let's grab a few winks of sleep. I'm tired."

Hardly had they tumbled into bed than they were sleeping heavily. There was not a sound in the great house save the *click-clack* of the grandfather's clock by the staircase.

Suddenly, from somewhere outside, there came a muffled cry. Again and again it was repeated.

Joe stirred slightly in his sleep, then lay silent. Frank's deep breathing continued.

The muffled cry ceased abruptly.

CHAPTER XVIII

EMERGING from the house, Fenton Hardy peered through the darkness with an expression of annoyance.

"Where on earth has Smalley gone? Running away from a couple of boys! Shucks!"

The detective strolled onto the broad, moonlit lawn.

"Smalley!" he called softly.

The rustling of the breeze in the trees was his only answer. He sauntered toward the street.

"Smalley!"

He listened intently. Was that a faint sound on the other side of the hedge? Mr. Hardy stiffened, every sense alert. Then with a sharp cry he whirled about.

He was an instant too late. A hurtling figure had crashed into him, knocking him flat.

"I guess you've monkeyed around just about enough," snarled a menacing voice as a steely fist closed around the detective's throat.

Fenton Hardy struggled desperately but to no avail. Finally he lay still.

"That's better," rasped the stranger. "No use wastin' your strength. We've caught up with you, Mr. Famous Detective!'' The man laughed hoarsely. ''We've been watchin' every move you've made for weeks. We know all about you.''

''Well?'' demanded Mr. Hardy. ''What do you want?''

''You know what I want, Fenton Hardy. Where's that book of records belonging to the Great States Company? Come on, speak up. Where is it?''

The detective said nothing. He felt the grip on his throat tighten.

''Where's that ledger?'' roared the man as the captive struggled to get his breath.

Whirling spots danced before Mr. Hardy's eyes. Then, just as he felt himself lapsing into unconsciousness, the hand around his neck loosened abruptly. Dimly the detective was aware of a newcomer.

''I've got him, Mr. Hardy,'' exclaimed a familiar voice.

There was a dull thud, followed by sounds of a struggle. Then came a shout, and the patter of running footsteps.

''He got away,'' groaned the familiar voice.

The detective pulled himself up with an effort. ''Oh, it's you, Smalley.''

''Yes, sir. I thought I had him. Hit him over the head with a blackjack, but when I turned around to look at you he jumped up and ran off.''

Fenton Hardy mopped his brow. ''Well,

never mind, Smalley. Only next time don't disappear when I need you. Didn't you recognize my sons?"

The guard looked at his chief questioningly. "Your sons, sir? I haven't seen them. For an hour I've been chasing the fellow that attacked you all over the place."

"Hmph. So that's the situation. Well, keep on watch, Smalley. Call me if you need me."

Mr. Hardy in deep thought returned to the house. Early next morning he told Frank at the breakfast table what had happened.

"So it *wasn't* the guard we ran after!" his son exclaimed. "It was somebody belonging to Hinchman's g——"

"Dad! Frank!" cried Joe, running into the room, his face chalk white. "The book of records is gone!"

"What!" exclaimed Mr. Hardy as he jumped to his feet, while Frank stared at his brother in dismay.

"The ledger's gone! Didn't we leave it on your desk last night, Dad?"

A hasty search of the entire house confirmed Joe's statement. Utterly discouraged, the boys fell into chairs and stared at each other.

"There goes the best evidence we had to convict Hinchman and his mob," Frank moaned. "We're right back where we started."

"Maybe we can remember some of the things we read in the book and write them down," Joe suggested.

"That wouldn't do any good. We'd have to produce the original ledger in court. Confound it all—it's our fault. We should have caught that fellow we scared off last night."

"We certainly should have. He's the one who took the book, no doubt about it."

"Or an accomplice," said Frank.

Fenton Hardy, who had gone to answer the telephone, came into the room just then. "Boys, I have received a call from the Justice Department in Washington. They want me there right away to confer on some matters. I'm relying on you to take care of the trucking case in my absence."

Promising that they would do their best, the brothers drove their father to the airport where the detective departed on an express plane. On the way home Frank bought a newspaper.

"Look at these headlines, Joe! Hinchman's operating again."

Excitedly Joe Hardy leaned over his brother's shoulder. " 'Shipment Worth Thousands Stolen at Bayport Wharf!' " he read aloud. "What do you think of that, Frank? They're working right here in Bayport!"

"*Were* working, you mean," groaned his brother. "By this time they're a long distance from here, no doubt."

"Unless they've hidden the stuff and will pick it up later, after the excitement dies down," offered Joe. "Shall we do some investigating?"

No sooner had they started than they ran into Chet Morton. Their chum was red-faced and panting.

"You're just the people I want to see," he cried excitedly. "I've caught one of your thieves!" he announced proudly. "But I wouldn't go through that again for a million dollars!"

"Go through what? Chet! What do you mean? Are you serious?" cried the Hardys.

"I was never more serious in my life," replied the stout boy. "You fellows have been so swell about the play, bringing swords and everything, that I thought I'd help you out in one of your mysteries. So when I read in the paper that a fellow named Castillo——"

"Castillo!" exclaimed Frank.

"Yes, the advertisement said Señor Castillo —he has just come to Bayport—would give fencing lessons."

"Don't tell me *you* went and had a fencing lesson!" exclaimed Joe, who, despite the fact that he could hardly wait for the rest of the story, found it hard not to laugh.

Chet looked hurt. "Gee, you fellows don't appreciate me helping to solve your old mystery at all," he complained.

"Please go on," pleaded Frank. "You'll admit you never showed any interest in playing with swords. What did you find out?"

"While Castillo was giving me a lesson, I asked him lots of questions," explained Chet.

"Whether he was a bullfighter and if he had a matador's sword and things like that."

"Gee, what did he say?" urged Joe.

"He isn't and he wasn't and he hasn't," grinned Chet.

"But I thought you said you had caught the thief," said Frank.

"I have," declared Chet, pausing. He was enjoying holding the upper hand in the conversation.

"Come on, tell us!" begged Frank.

"This fencing Castillo told me that the matador Castillo is working at a circus!" Chet announced. "He doesn't know which one, but that ought to make it easy for you fellows," the fat boy concluded.

The Hardys almost hugged their chum. "Gee, you're wonderful," Joe praised him. "What can we do for you right now to show our appreciation?"

Chet wiped his perspiring brow and rolled his tongue in his mouth. "You can buy me a quart of ice cream and take me out in your *Sleuth* while I eat it!" he grinned.

"You deserve that—at least," laughed Frank, and Joe agreed.

Half an hour later the three were on board the *Sleuth*. While Joe cast off the mooring, Frank at the helm guided the trim craft out into the choppy waters of the harbor and thence into the wide spaces of Barmet Bay.

"Golly, isn't that breeze great?" exclaimed

Chet in delight. "This is the life!" he added, dipping a spoon into a box of vanilla ice cream.

"What's that off the starboard bow, Frank?" interrupted Joe. "Looks like an old fishing schooner."

His brother brought out the binoculars and gazed through them for several moments. "It is a schooner called the *Mirador*. And there's another boat alongside. A big motor cruiser," he informed the others.

"That's odd. Can you make out what they're doing?"

"Why, they don't seem to be doing anyth— yes, they are! They're transferring some boxes from the schooner to the cruiser. There goes one—two—three—hold the *Sleuth* steady, Joe!" Frank continued his intent gaze while his brother slowed down the motorboat's engine.

"There," said the older boy a moment later. "Six boxes in all. They seem to be finished. The cruiser is leaving."

Joe and Chet could see the smaller vessel edge off from the other and finally turn toward shore. At the same time the huge mainsail of the schooner rose majestically, followed by the foresail, jumbo and jib. Then the ship put out toward sea.

"What do you think it all means, Frank?" Joe queried tensely.

"It looks like stealing. Cargo isn't transferred offshore when there's a good wharf as close as Bayport. I think we ought to follow the small boat and find out what we can."

Chet made a face. "Just when we were having a nice, pleasant trip, too. You'll never catch that boat. She's almost out of sight now."

"Look out, here comes a wave!" Joe sang out.

The *Sleuth* was tossed about in the choppy water. In a moment all three boys were drenched with flying spray. Frank eased the throttle somewhat. As he did so a giant wave crashed into them, all but overturning the little craft. Chet uttered a cry.

"Hey! What are you trying to do, Frank, drown us?" he shouted. "I thought we came out for a good time."

The *Sleuth* lurched again as a huge comber bore down on them, spewing foam across the reeling deck. Joe peered around.

"I'm afraid we're in for a bad time, Frank," he observed. "The wind's getting stronger every minute."

Frank nodded. "I guess we'll have to go back, worse luck."

After a rough half-hour the *Sleuth* entered the comparative calm of the Bayport harbor and at length drew up to its dock. The Hardys drove Chet home, thanked him again for his tip about the matador, then went to their own house.

"Let's call Dad and tell him what we saw,"

suggested Frank. "Maybe he'll have some ideas."

He waited until he was sure his father had arrived in Washington, then telephoned him at the Department of Justice, relating their adventure.

"What did he say?" his brother queried eagerly, as Frank hung up.

"That schooner called the *Mirador* is due at Ocean Bluff tonight with a valuable cargo of silk for a parachute company. He wants us to be there when it arrives. Says what we saw might have been stolen from the shipment."

"Ocean Bluff's only ten miles away," said Frank. "We'll just about make it before the ship does if we hurry."

They reached the Ocean Bluff wharf in good time, and soon spied the old vessel nosing toward the pier, using its auxiliary engine. Frank pulled his brother into the shadows.

"We'd better not be seen," he warned.

It seemed an eternity before the boat was made fast to the dock a few yards from where the Hardys were hiding. Suddenly a big van drove up. Its driver jumped out and approached a man who appeared to be the schooner's captain.

"I'm from the parachute company," announced the employee, showing some papers. "Fifteen crates."

"They're on deck," the captain barked, returning the papers. "Go ahead and get 'em, and make it snappy."

Tensely the boys counted the boxes as the driver carried them to his vehicle.

"Nine boxes," whispered Joe at length. "Six to go."

"What's the matter? He's quitting. There he goes to talk with the captain."

The man's words were distinctly audible. "Where are the rest of the boxes, Cap'n? Six more."

The boys could see the officer frown. "Who says six more? I told you all your boxes were on deck."

"But they ain't all there, Cap."

"Then they weren't loaded on. That's all I've got."

Joe nudged his brother. "Listen to that, Frank! Let's go tell the old fuss-pot what we know about him."

Before Frank could restrain him Joe had stepped up to the two men.

CHAPTER XIX

THE CIRCUS

"CAPTAIN, we saw you transfer six boxes from your schooner to a cruiser about two hours ago," declared Joe Hardy boldly.

"What's that? Who might you be, you young rapscallion? Why, I'll pull your ears and——"

"What's all the rumpus?" demanded a new voice.

A tall policeman stepped up. Quickly Joe explained the situation and offered to telephone to the original loading point of the cargo. He did this and found that fifteen cases of parachute silk had been placed on the schooner originally.

"You'd better come along to the station house, Captain," ordered the policeman when Joe reported his findings. "Sounds like something phony goin' on."

Despite the angry protests of the schooner's officer he was led off, while the parachute company driver thanked Joe.

"Much obliged, fellows," he said. "You certainly are clever. You ought to be detectives."

The Hardys laughed, said they were glad to have been of help, and returned home.

"Hello, what's this?" exclaimed Frank as the boys walked into their living room. "Hm. Letter from Mr. Webster."

"Maybe it's good news about Narvey," replied Joe. "Hurry up and open it."

His brother did so, and unruffled a large sheet of paper covered with sprawling letters.

"Not much good news," was his answer. "Mr. Webster says his son, who is worse, keeps referring to Moe Gordon. Narvey's father says he'll give us a huge reward if we can catch the crook, because he thinks the young man never will be cured until that fellow is behind bars."

Joe regarded his brother thoughtfully. "A lot of people will be better off, Frank, if we can catch Gordon—and Hinchman—and Storch, too."

"While we're waiting to hear further orders from Dad, why don't we concentrate on circuses?" suggested his brother. "I'd like to follow up Chet's clue to the stolen estoque."

"I should, too," said Joe. "Oh, good, there goes the dinner bell. We'd better wash ourselves and comb our hair before Aunt Gertrude sees us," he laughed.

A few minutes later the three sat down to a delicious soup course.

"I'm glad you're here," sighed Aunt Gertrude. "I get tired of eating alone. Your mother in one place, your father in another, and you two off risking your lives. I never saw such a family!"

"I'm glad we're here, too," said Joe. A few minutes later he exclaimed, "Aunt Gertrude, this is the best soup I've ever tasted."

The old lady beamed. Apparently she had either forgotten about the sword episode or else had forgiven her nephews for scaring her.

"You boys must be hungry after all your running around. I do wish you would stay at home more. Some day something dreadful will —" she began.

Frank jumped to answer the ringing telephone. After a considerable interval he returned, winked at Joe but continued eating. When the meal was over he drew his brother into their father's study.

"That was Dad, Joe. He wants us to meet him tomorrow afternoon at a circus being held at Summit. Says he has important news."

"At the *circus?*" gulped Joe. "What on earth does he want us to meet him there for?"

"I don't know. But maybe we'll find the matador Castillo and the stolen estoque, too, while we're doing a job for Dad."

Joe nodded. "And Mr. Webster's home is on the way there. Why don't we get up early so that we can stop at High Point?"

"We'll have to leave so early we won't get

much sleep," complained Frank. "I'd rather go part of the distance tonight."

Joe grinned. "Aunt Gertrude will be hurt if we leave her this evening."

"You're right," agreed his brother. "Let's play some game with her—we'll let her choose it—and then we'll start off about four in the morning."

The old lady bubbled over with delight, and later, after a great deal of fun, said she had not had such a good time in months. The boys got off promptly at a very early hour and set out for High Point. By nine o'clock they were standing on the front porch of the Webster mansion.

"What a place!" Frank exclaimed. "Flower gardens, greenhouses, stables——"

"Come in, gentlemen," greeted a jovial-looking Negro butler, opening the door just then.

When the elderly millionaire came to shake hands with the boys, they were shocked at the look on his face. He appeared very worried and unhappy.

"I'm so glad you are here," he said in a quavering voice. "Narvey is—is worse. The specialist holds out no hope for his mind being restored. It is breaking my heart."

"May we see him?" Frank asked kindly.

"Certainly, boys. I am eager that you should. He keeps muttering the name of Moe Gordon to himself over and over. He seems to have a deadly fear of the man. Tell me, is that crook still at large?"

Joe nodded. "We are doing everything possible to catch him, Mr. Webster."

Mr. Webster smiled faintly. "I am glad. Only I hope you succeed in time. I am confident that if Gordon is imprisoned my boy will recover. Come upstairs. We shall visit him."

The Hardys followed the man up a long, winding staircase and down a hall.

"Here is his room. Go right in."

Frank's heart skipped a beat as he pushed open the door. There, huddled on the bed, was a figure which was the very picture of despair.

"Narvey!" Frank called softly. "Narvey, we're Frank and Joe Hardy!"

For a long moment the young man remained motionless. Then, very slowly, he turned toward them.

"Narvey, don't you remember us?" Joe urged.

"Yes, I remember," came the answer. "And you were going to catch Moe Gordon. But you haven't. You haven't. He still haunts me!" The poor fellow began to sob, then broke into a wild laugh. "He eats cheese all the time. I hate cheese! I hate him! But I can't get away from him!"

The Hardys looked at each other. "I think we'd better leave," murmured Frank.

Mr. Webster nodded and they all filed out. "You see, he is much worse," said the father sadly when they reached his study.

Frank and Joe were forced to agree with him. "But we'll redouble our efforts to trap Moe Gordon," they promised.

Sympathetically they bade the broken-hearted man good-bye and drove off.

"You know, Frank, I'm not certain we've figured out Narvey's case yet," said Joe. "There's something mighty strange about the whole situation."

"Funny, but I've had the same feeling. Is the fellow going insane or by any chance has Gordon been here bothering him?"

"From Narvey's words, one could certainly think that the crook has been," agreed Joe. "Or else Narvey *thinks* Gordon is around."

"Do you think we ought to notify the police to keep an eye on this place?" asked Frank.

"Let's wait a little while," suggested his brother. "Poor Mr. Webster has had so much trouble already. He probably does not want any further publicity."

For a good part of the remainder of the ride to the circus both were silent, each wrapped in his own thoughts. They listened to the radio for a while, then stopped for lunch. At last a signpost announced that Summit was only a mile away.

"Here we are," said Joe.

"I can hardly wait to see Dad," added Frank as they neared the city. "I've been curious about what news he may have for us."

"How are we supposed to find him in the midst of a circus? He didn't tell you where he'd be, did he?"

Frank shook his head. "You know Dad's methods, Joe. He doesn't give much information over a phone. Don't worry, he'll see to it that we find him."

The circus grounds were not hard to locate, for a large ferris wheel was visible for some distance. Covering several acres around the giant structure were gaily decorated tents. Swarms of people were about.

"Get the admission tickets while I park the car," said Frank excitedly.

A few moments later the brothers strolled arm in arm into the noisy area. At once Joe exclaimed, "Look at the side shows! Let's go into one."

His brother smilingly shook his head. "Later. We'd better find Dad first. It's after three now."

The boys pushed their way through the crowds surging among the tents and food stands but saw no sign of the detective.

"Balloons? Balloons? Buy a balloon?" squawked a rough-looking vendor, jostling them rudely.

Impatiently the boys pushed the fellow aside

and continued their stroll. To their annoyance the man rushed after them, all but knocking them over in his persistence.

"Hey, fellas! Buy a balloon! Only a nickel!"

"We don't want a balloon!" replied Frank with an emphatic gesture, but when he endeavored to push past the man the latter blocked his way.

"It looks as if we'll have to call out the Reserves to get rid of this fellow," said Joe under his breath. "If you don't mind," he added aloud, "we aren't the least bit interested in your balloons."

"No?" The vendor's face bore a hurt expression. "You no likea my balloon? You no wanta buy for some poor leetle kiddies? Look, I show you something special!"

Despite the boys' irritation their curiosity got the better of them. The man had transferred his string of toys to one hand while he fumbled in a torn pocket with the other. As Frank and Joe watched mystified, the vendor drew forth a crumpled sheet of paper which he held toward them.

"What's this?" snorted Joe, staring at the man.

Suddenly his jaw dropped. He started to utter an exclamation but caught himself and reached for the paper.

"Come on, Frank," he whispered, pulling his astounded brother through the crowd and off to one side. "Didn't you recognize him? What a disguise. Why, even Mother wouldn't have known Dad!"

"Let's see what his note says. 'Dear Boys:' Try to get jobs with circus. Important. Meet me at main gate at closing time. Will explain later. Love, Dad.' "

The openmouthed astonishment of the boys quickly gave way to determination to follow their disguised parent's instructions. They would ask questions later.

"We'll probably have better luck if we separate," suggested Joe. "I'll go down there by that snake pen and see what luck I have."

"All right. Meet you later."

Frank watched his brother disappear through the crowd, then strolled toward a large open-sided tent containing a number of elephants. A keeper was engaged in feeding the animals. On a sudden impulse Frank Hardy stepped up to him.

"Pardon me, but could you by any chance give me a job helping you?"

The man whirled around. "You thinka you can feed elephants, young fellah?"

"I believe I can. I've been watching you."

"How much mon' you wanta get pay?"

Frank hid a smile and shrugged. "Oh, anything. Not much. Anything you want to pay."

The bronzed, rugged keeper looked at Frank dubiously. "You might get stepped on. Well, be verra careful. Go to the main office tent.

Tell 'em Mike here senda you. Tell 'em I need extra fellah.''

Thanking the keeper, Frank hurried through the throng and found his way to a large tent near the entrance. A man in shirt sleeves looked up as he entered.

"Well?"

"I'd like a job, sir. Mike over at the elephant tent sent me here. He said he'd take me on."

"Hmph. Gettin' lazy in his old age, is he? Needs more help, does he? Well, all right. Come back here tonight for your pay."

On his way back Frank kept a sharp lookout for any familiar faces. "There's a good chance that some of Hinchman's pals are here, otherwise Dad wouldn't have sent for us," he decided.

Yet he saw no sign of him or Gordon. Arriving at the elephant tent he was handed a large pail of water.

"Keepa out the way their tusks," warned Mike. "Jest hold the pail tight and keepa your arms and hands away."

"How does one hold a pail without using one's arms and hands?" the boy chuckled to himself.

Nevertheless he went to work, refilling the pail at intervals as the elephants emptied it. At the same time he was alert to the remarks of the swarming bystanders in case one of them should turn out to be a suspicious character.

"Here, boy, give him some peanuts," called a voice in the crowd.

"Nothing doing," snorted Mike, who happened to be standing at hand. "Don't takea no peanuts from the crowd," he warned Frank. "Whata you think?" he added, turning toward the onlookers. "My elephants get enough to eat."

Laughing to himself, Frank finally completed his rounds. His muscles aching, he put down the heavy pail and stood watching the crowd pressing around the rail. Suddenly he stiffened.

"That fellow looks familiar," he said tensely to himself.

The man whom his quick eye had picked out was dressed in expensive clothes and apparently had had a recent shave and haircut.

"I know! Hinchman!" flashed across Frank's brain. "Golly, I almost didn't recognize him all spruced up! Or is he Hinchman?" He stared at the man doubtfully. "It's either he or his double!"

Just then the fellow turned away and was swallowed up in the crowd.

CHAPTER XX

THE MATADOR'S SWORD

FRANK took a step forward. Should he attempt to follow Hinchman? The ex-candy store owner already was out of sight.

"Wassa matter?" cackled a voice just then. "You no got anything to do? Here, start cleaning the place." It was Mike. The humorous keeper handed Frank a huge mop. "You no lay down on the job so soon, no?"

The boy's first impulse was to fling away the mop and run after the person he thought was Hinchman. An instant later he realized how foolish such a move would be.

"I'll wait," he said to himself. "Sooner or later——"

Out of the corner of his eye he caught sight of a familiar face. Pretending not to notice his brother who came up just then, he walked casually toward the elephant nearest the rail.

"What's up, Frank? See anything suspicious?" came a whisper.

"I just saw Hinchman, Joe. At least I think so. All dressed up in sporty tweeds," the older boy whispered out of the corner of his mouth.

Observing Mike watching him from the other side of the elephant pen, Frank began working busily with the mop. Joe edged closer.

"That was the crook's brother," he said. "He's called Big Top Hinchman. Owns the circus. I found out all about him."

"Sh. Here comes Mike."

"See you at closing time," whispered Joe.

Impatiently the boy kept on as the hours dragged by. Finally he glanced at his watch with a sigh of relief. It was two minutes before midnight.

"All right, go get your money," said Mike, stepping up.

Without further ado young Hardy hurried through the departing crowd to the main office tent, where he collected his wages. Then he lingered about the entrance gate in the shadows.

"Frank! That you?" A hand was placed on the boy's shoulder in the darkness.

"Hello, Joe! Where's Dad?"

"Coming. Here he is now."

Silently the detective and his two sons clasped hands. Mr. Hardy had removed all make-up and looked like his real self.

"What shall we do now, Dad?" Frank whispered tensely.

"Look around a little, as soon as the last of the crowd leaves. Ah, the lights are out. I think we shall go for a casual stroll through the grounds."

Their father led them to a narrow path behind the tents that bordered the edge of the circus plot.

"I think it would be unwise to walk along the

main paths. Keep your eyes and ears open, boys.''

The detective suddenly seemed to freeze in his tracks. He appeared to be staring at some object in the blackness. Then he motioned to his sons.

''Crouch low and follow me, boys,'' were his words.

Wonderingly the brothers crawled through a patch of tall grass. A large canvas loomed directly ahead of them. The entrance flap was up, so they could look inside.

''It's the snake tent,'' breathed Joe into Frank's ear. ''That's where I was working this afternoon.''

Mr. Hardy halted suddenly. A tense silence followed. Then came a queer, scraping sound.

''I can't see a thing. What's going on?'' whispered Joe, who was behind the other two.

Frank repeated the question to his father. The latter cupped his hands to Frank's ear and whispered, ''Somebody's trying to break the lock on the snakes' cage. Look slightly to the left. See?''

His son's eyes fell on a bulky shadow crouched directly in front of what appeared to be a barred door. The scraping sound continued. There was a loud *snap* followed by a grunt.

''Sh. Don't make a move,'' Mr. Hardy warned the boys almost soundlessly. ''Someone's coming.''

As footsteps approached the tent, the crouched figure suddenly glided away. A new form loomed up. It was a watchman. He walked past the cage, and likewise disappeared. For several moments the detective and his sons remained motionless.

"All right, I think we're safe," said Fenton Hardy at length. "One of you go up and see what you find at the cage door."

"I'll go," whispered Frank, and stole to the barred entrance. It seemed to his brother as if he were gone for an eternity, but finally he reappeared, very excited. "Look! Part of a sword blade! It must have broken off while that man was trying to open the lock with it."

"Is it a piece of the Crusader's sword?" whispered Joe.

"It's too dark to see."

"We'll examine it later," said Mr. Hardy. "We must get away from here without being seen."

After tediously crawling on hands and knees the three reached the street fence. Quickly scaling it, they hurried to their cars and departed for a hotel where the detective had engaged rooms. At once the group began to examine the piece of weapon Frank had found.

"Golly, it *is* part of Mr. Barker's sword!" exclaimed the boy. "See, it says 'P O I N.' Now we have the last name of the knight. 'P O I N-C E L O T.' "

"If we recover the piece with his first name, we'll probably discover the thief who stole the money from Mr. Barker's office,'' said Joe. ''I'm relieved to know the rest of the blade wasn't buried in the warehouse wreckage.''

''And I'm sorry we didn't nab that fellow to-night,'' added the boys' father. ''In my zeal to obtain conclusive proof, I'm afraid I let one of the trucking thieves slip through my fingers. Well, we'll have to renew our efforts.''

In the morning the brothers separated from their father, promising to meet him at the main gate of the circus at midnight.

''Before we go to work, let's find out if a man named Castillo who used to be a bullfighter is with this show,'' suggested Frank.

''Good idea,'' said Joe. ''I'll find a program.'' He picked one from a trash basket. His eyes grew large as he skimmed through the list of names. ''Here is one,'' he said. '' 'Señor Castillo, Expert Aerialist.' ''

''Let's hunt up the man right away,'' cried Frank. ''Of course we'll have to be careful how we go about questioning him.''

The boys found the small, handsome, dark man in his dressing room, trying on a new suit for his act. He looked like anything but a thief as he stood there in a white satin shirt and tight-fitting breeches!

''You like heem—my new clothes?'' the performer smiled as the Hardys entered. ''He is better than the last one. Now when I am way up at top the tent on my trapeze, everyone can see Señor Castillo,'' he added with pride.

''That will be good,'' smiled Frank. ''Such

a fine actor as you should have the spotlight,"
he added, realizing the fellow liked flattery.

The man beamed. "That ees correct. **And**
now what can I do for you boys?"

"We're new here—just started working yesterday," spoke up Joe. "Thought we'd get
acquainted with the circus people."

"Have you always been a trapeze performer?" asked Frank.

"Oh, no, no," came the quick reply. "In the
native land Señor Castillo was a great matador!
But alas, there is no money—no more money
in my poor country for the famous bullfighter.
The war! The taxes! Oh, thees horrible thing
they do to the great artist!"

The temperamental man had to stop speaking
for lack of breath. The Hardys were tingling
with excitement. Perhaps they were talking
with the very person who had Mr. Barker's
stolen estoque!

"Have you kept the sword you used when you
were a bullfighter?" asked Frank, trying not to
show any undue interest in the subject.

"Sí, sí, but he is not in this country," Castillo
answered. "Never would I part with heem,
but he is no use here. So I leave heem home."

The brothers wondered what they might say
next, for they were not gleaning the information they wanted. At last Frank decided to
take a bold step.

"We know a man who has a wonderful collection of swords," he ventured. Castillo

showed no special interest. "One of them is a matador's," the boy added, watching the actor closely. Still no sign of guilt on the face of this man, who continued to admire himself in a mirror. "It has been stolen!" cried the boy.

"That ees too bad," said Castillo, not even flicking an eyelash. "You will excuse me now. I change my clothes. You are nice boys. Come again sometime. Then I show you my new estoque. I just get heem. He is beautiful."

At this announcement the Hardys nearly gave themselves away. Only because of long training with their father were they able to hide the excitement they felt.

"Oh, please show it to us now," begged Joe, trying to appear as innocent in his desire as a pleading child. *"Please!"*

"You will be late to work," laughed the performer. "Then the Big Top Hinch-a-man, he be mad. But I show you."

The man opened a trunk and reached to the bottom of it. In a second he was displaying a fine, short sword with a beautiful jeweled hilt. At once the Hardys recognized it, from the photograph they had seen, as belonging to Mr. Barker.

"Oh!" cried both boys together.

"You exclaim!" laughed the ex-matador. "No wonder. He is very gorgeous, sí, sí."

Convinced that this man had obtained possession of the estoque by honest means, the brothers disliked having to tell him the truth.

For several seconds no one spoke. Over the actor's head Frank moved his lips soundlessly to form the words, "Shall we tell him?" Joe nodded to go ahead.

"Señor Castillo," Frank began, "would you mind telling us where you got this sword?"

"I buy heem—from some man. I do not know thees man. One day I tell heem I would like to buy a beautiful estoque some time. Bye-m-bye he come back with thees one."

"I am afraid you will have to give it up," said Joe as kindly as possible. "Unfortunately this is the sword which was taken from the collection my brother told you about a few minutes ago. The man who sold it to you stole it!"

Castillo turned white, then red. "What you say! *Caramba!* Stole it! And I pay heem so much money! All my one week salary!" Like an angry animal the matador paced the room a few seconds, then stopped short. "Who are you boys? You do not tell the truth! Get out!" he cried.

Seizing the estoque which he had laid on a table he began brandishing it, then held it in front of him as if he were about to stab an onrushing bull. Frightened, the boys ran from the tent, the cry ringing in their ears, "*Caramba!* One week salary to a thief. No, no, it cannot be. I feex those boys."

"What'll we do now?" gasped Joe, when he and his brother were a safe distance away. "Wow, is he mad!"

"I know what I'll do," laughed Frank. "Hide in the elephant's pen till Castillo cools off!"

"Guess I better go about my work, too," said Joe. "Well, see you later. It's great having found Mr. Barker's sword, isn't it?"

"Chet really did help solve that mystery," added Frank. "We'll have to buy him more than a quart of ice cream for his good work."

"We might get him a fencing foil," Joe grinned as he moved off.

He hurried down a path toward the snake cage. As he passed one of the small tents, he heard a loud voice that made him stop in his tracks.

"You want to use our supply headquarters for a warehouse, you say?" queried the voice.

On impulse the boy crept up to the flap and peered inside. He suppressed an exclamation as he recognized Big Top Hinchman with his mouth glued to a telephone.

"You say the explosion wrecked your place, Charlie?" A staccato sound crackled through the receiver. Then Big Top spoke again. "Well, all right, you can use our circus storage warehouse for a while. What's that? Sure, we'll need it later."

The receiver was banged back on the hook.

"Hm," mused Joe, his pulses quickening. "Here's a real clue to Hinchman and those other thieves. I wonder if Big Top knows what they're up to?"

CHAPTER XXI

A CLOWN'S STORY

DECIDING this bit of news was worth communicating to his brother at once, Joe hurried to the elephants' pen. The keeper was not around, so the boys could talk freely.

"Gee, you certainly did get a clue," agreed Frank after he had heard Joe's story. "Dad ought to be told."

"Guess we can't do that until midnight," said Joe. "In the meantime we ought to try to find out where the supply headquarters of the circus is located."

"That ought to be easy," commented Frank. "Any of the people working here can tell us, only we'd better not seem too interested. Somebody might become suspicious. I'll ask Mike when he gets back."

The boys separated, Joe going to the snake tent. The elephants' keeper soon returned. He beamed broadly at Frank.

"Here you are, my lad! Plenty heavy work, yes?"

"Elephants eat an awful lot, don't they?" remarked the boy. "Where do you get their feed? It must cost a circus a good deal."

"Big Top Hinchman—he own a storage

place in Willowside. Only about one day trip from here. Not bad, eh? He buy wholesale, keep stuff there."

With that Mike was off to give orders to some of his other helpers loitering about. Grinning to himself Frank worked hard, not forgetting to keep one eye on the crowd for possible suspicious faces. Early in the evening the superintendent of the circus appeared on his round of inspection.

"Hello," he said with a friendly wave of his hand. "How are you getting along?"

"Very well, thank you, Mr. Smith," Frank replied.

"How would you and your brother like to knock off work for the rest of the day and see the performance with me?" the man asked. "I want to watch part of the show tonight and I'd like company."

Frank needed no second invitation. Rounding up Joe and informing him of the treat in store, they set off. A short time later they joined the superintendent and soon were watching the exciting and dangerous feats of the aerial troupe.

"Isn't that Señor Castillo up there on the trapeze?" asked Frank. "The man who has on a white satin suit?"

"Yes, it is," replied Mr. Smith. "Excellent performer."

Openmouthed, the boys watched the skill and grace of Castillo and the other two men with him. Each stunt seemed more miraculous and breath-taking than the preceding one.

"Do you think you could turn three somersaults in mid-air like that, Frank?" laughed Joe.

"One would do," replied his brother. "Although I have done a double one diving into the water," he added.

"Do you boys go in for a lot of athletics?" asked Mr. Smith.

"We do as much as we can," replied Joe. "At High School we're members of a gymnasium club, which has given a few exhibitions."

Finally, when the show ended, the boys sighed disappointedly.

"I could watch that all night, Mr. Smith," said Joe to the superintendent. "Thank you so much for letting us off from work and inviting us here."

Shortly after midnight, as the lights of the circus grounds were extinguished, the boys found their father waiting for them near the entrance.

"Any plans?" Joe queried.

"Nothing special. I'm wondering whether you boys have anything to report?"

"Plenty, Dad," whispered Joe tensely, telling the story of the discovery of the stolen estoque.

"Fine work," the detective praised his sons. "You should let Mr. Barker know about this right away."

"You don't think Castillo may get rid of the sword?" asked Joe.

"Not if he's honest, and from what you tell me, I'm sure he is," replied the boy's father.

"We have some other news, even more important to you," said Frank. "Hinchman is going to store his stuff in Big Top's headquarters at Willowside!"

At this announcement Mr. Hardy actually hugged his sons. "Wonderful!" he exclaimed. "I'll go there and check up."

"When?" Frank asked.

"Tomorrow morning. I don't know when I shall return, but I'll be in touch with you."

He was gone the next day by the time the boys arose and prepared for their work at the circus. Arriving at the grounds they were told the superintendent wanted to see them.

"Wonder what's up?" said Frank. "Hope he hasn't found out our real reason for being here."

What the man had to say was a great surprise indeed.

"Good morning, boys," he boomed, grasping each of them by a hand and leading them toward the office tent. "I have an offer for both of you."

The boys' eyes opened wide. Expectantly they waited for the man's next words.

"It seems that three of my acrobats have been taken ill. Food poisoning. I recall what you told me last night about your gymnastic work. I'm wondering if you could pinch-hit for two of the performers. I have a man here who can do the work of the third.''

"You want *us* to—take the places of the other two?" Joe asked incredulously.

"Yes, that is my offer. At this time of the season I can get no trained acrobats as substitutes. I have only two alternatives. Either I must skip the act entirely, or use you boys.''

Frank's eyes flashed. "We'll be glad to help you," he said eagerly.

Out of the corner of his eye he could see Joe's jaw dropping in surprise. But the younger lad was just as game as his brother.

"Good. The first show isn't until two o'clock this afternoon. Go over to the tent now and you'll have two hours to rehearse.''

Conferring excitedly, the boys hurried away. As they entered the big tent, a pang went through Frank. "There's Castillo, Joe. Guess he's the other substitute. Do you suppose he has forgiven us yet?" he whispered.

It was soon evident that the former bullfighter had not forgotten his grievance. Informed that the boys were to take part in the show, he exploded in a volley of words the boys could not understand. It took the combined efforts of the other performers to quiet him.

"Well, all right, I behave," he said sullenly. "But one week salary—he gone to a thief! Now you boys practice. I watch you fall off the trapeze, yes?" he laughed.

Soon the rehearsal was progressing in earnest. To everyone's delight the brothers did remarkably well. The regular performers changed their act a little to suit the ability of the Hardys but were amazed at the lads' skill.

"All right, that ees enough for now," said Castillo at length. "Go rest and be back here by two o'clock for the main show."

Tingling with anticipation, the boys walked up and down the circus grounds until the appointed hour. When they entered the big tent again it was literally jammed with spectators.

"Nervous, Joe?"

"A little. I wouldn't mind so much if we weren't working with Castillo. He's still upset—and temperamental. No telling what he may do."

When it was time for their act, the band blared forth. The Hardys climbed to a trapeze. The first stunts went all right. Then came the moment for the difficult one. Señor Castillo, swinging above the others by his heels, awaited word from the announcer.

"L-a-d-e-e-z and gentlemun," called the ringmaster in stentorian tones. "Introducing a new and daring act! You will now see one somersault after another in lightning succession."

As the drums rolled the three regular actors turned in the air, caught Castillo's hands, and swung back to their trapezes.

"Ready?" snapped Castillo to Frank.

"Ready!" called the boy, bracing himself.

He flipped over, missed the Señor, and tumbled headlong into the net. The crowd booed, and the boy flushed furiously.

As he watched in anguish, his brother met the same fate, landing in the great net. Again the vast crowd roared its disgust. Climbing to the ground, Joe joined his brother.

"It wasn't our fault, Frank, it was Castillo's," the younger boy said angrily. "He deliberately timed his swing so he couldn't catch hold!"

"Joe, let's do that somersault stunt we did at the last gym club show at high school."

"Just give me a chance!" agreed his brother. "Come on, we'll show Señor Castillo and everybody else just what we can do."

At this point one of the clowns, who had overheard the remark, paused in his antics. When Frank and Joe started their act, to the surprise of the announcer and Castillo, the funny man joined the boys. What might have been just a clever but plain acrobatic performance on the part of the Hardys now turned into an amazing and sidesplitting number. The audience clapped and howled its approval, asking for an encore.

"You ought to join us permanently," said the clown as the three bowed and walked off. "Say, come on into my dressing room for a while. I'd like to know you better."

Thanking the man for his helpfulness, the boys followed him into one of the dressing rooms at the rear of the tent. When the clown removed his costume he turned out to be a pleasant-faced young man to whom the boys took an instant liking.

"Do you mean to tell me you're just amateurs?" queried the clown incredulously. "Why, I've been knocking around circuses all my life and I supposed you were old-timers."

Joe chuckled. "I'll have to tell our gym teacher that. Incidentally, while you two fellows are talking, I think I'll run over and see how my snake pen is getting along. I told the keeper I'd take care of his job between shows."

Frank had been studying the young clown. Maybe the friendly man could give him some useful information in regard to Big Top's brother and his pals.

"Do any of the circus owner's relatives work here?" the boy asked to lead the conversation in that direction.

"Not any more," replied the clown. "One used to, but he had to leave. Big Top caught him stealing things and there was a big rumpus. It was hushed up, 'cause he was a cousin, so not many of the performers knew about it."

"What was his name?"

"Moe Gordon," came the startling reply. "I never liked him. Too free and easy with knives. Seemed to know a lot about them—and swords too."

Frank could hardly contain himself and was about to ask another leading question, when the clown made a further amazing announcement.

"I sure was sorry about one thing," he said. "We had a nice young trapeze performer here named Marko. That wasn't his right name. He never told me who he was, but I had an idea he was a rich man's son and had run away from home."

At once Frank's mind leaped to Narvey.

"Poor Marko fell and became lame," went on the clown. "After that he got in Gordon's clutches and had to leave, too. I'm afraid the poor fellow may have told the thief he has a wealthy father and been made to get money out of him for Gordon."

"Did this Marko suffer from loss of memory after his fall?" asked Frank.

"That I don't know," said the circus man. "But he certainly did act differently."

Before leaving to tell Joe what he had learned, Frank asked one more question. "Did Castillo know Gordon?"

The clown looked surprised but replied, "Castillo joined us just before Gordon was asked to leave, so I don't believe he did."

Thanking the friendly man again for his help in the acrobatic act, the Hardy boy left the tent. He almost bumped into his brother who was running toward him, wild-eyed.

"Something terrible has happened!" Joe yelled. "One of the poisonous snakes is missing!"

CHAPTER XXII

THE MISSING SNAKE

FRANK at once looked concerned. "That's bad! We'd better tell the superintendent, Joe. Somebody may be bitten."

The boys sought out Mr. Smith, who raced over to the snake tent with them. "Where's the head keeper?" the man cried. "Had no business leaving his job."

"How did you find out one snake was missing?" Frank asked his brother.

"When I fed them, I counted," Joe replied. "One was gone."

The superintendent glowered. "That's a fine how-do-ye-do! A viper loose! People wanderin' around!"

Frank, calmer, asked, "Don't you think we'd better look for the snake?"

"You bet we'd better start lookin', and that keeper is goin' to lose his job. Tony!" he shouted to a helper. "Go get the boss, quick!"

The circus owner was not long in arriving. Looking like a dapper sportsman in his natty tweeds he trotted up to them, his face livid.

"What's this I hear about a snake escaping?" he hissed.

"This young fellow here says one got away,"

growled the superintendent, motioning toward Joe. "A poisonous one at that."

"Good heavens, man, do you know what that means if the public should get wind of it?" cried Big Top Hinchman. "Nobody'll come to the show! Start a search of the grounds at once," the owner ordered. His voice dropped to a hoarse whisper. "Whatever you do, don't let the customers know what's going on."

The boys as well as the men hunted everywhere on the grounds but the missing reptile was not found. At last they gave it up. The Hardys drew off by themselves and began to discuss the many things they had found out during the past few hours.

"I believe that snake was stolen!" decided Joe. "The lock was tampered with, as we know. And it was done by the person with the broken blade of the Crusader's sword."

Frank slapped his knee. "I'll bet you that person is Moe Gordon!" he cried, and told Joe the clown's story. "Gordon's sore at Big Top and what better way to get back at him than to let a dangerous snake loose at a circus? Furthermore, the clown said Moe liked knives and swords, so he's probably the one who used the blade to open the cage."

"Your theory sounds good," said Joe. "And since two and two make four, Gordon is the one who sold the stolen estoque to Castillo."

"Yes, it looks as if our case is narrowing,"

agreed Frank. "Either Charlie Hinchman or Gordon took the piece of the Crusader's sword from Mr. Barker's office and the matador's estoque from his home, but Gordon probably is the one who had them later."

"Tell me again about the young man called Marko," asked Joe. "It certainly sounds as if he is Narvey."

Frank reiterated the clown's words, including the man's worry that the lame circus chap probably was under Gordon's influence still and might even be getting money in some way from a wealthy father to give to the crook.

"That would explain why Narvey's condition doesn't improve," he concluded. "If he is in constant fear of Gordon and is forced by him to ask his father for money, no wonder the poor fellow's mind is in a turmoil. That's enough to put a well person in a state of amnesia!"

"I think we ought to go out to High Point and have a talk with Mr. Webster," said Joe. "We can find out if Narvey called himself Marko. If so, he may even tell us that Gordon comes there. And this time we'll catch that thief!"

The boys decided to go the next day, so at midnight when they received their wages they said they would not be back to work in the morning. After a good sleep at the hotel, they telephoned their home. Mr. and Mrs. Hardy still were away, Aunt Gertrude reported. Her nephews asked her to tell their parents, if they should return, that the boys were going to the Webster home.

"More gallavantin'!" the woman said tartly. "I should think you'd want to come home for another good meal instead of eating restaurant food all the time!" With that she hung up the receiver.

Laughing, the brothers hurried to the hotel dining room for breakfast. Joe bought a morning newspaper and at once exclaimed over a prominent headline.

TRUCKING MOB ROUND-UP BEGUN

Frank uttered a whoop. "Look, Joe, here's Matty Storch's picture! And half a dozen other crooks. Dad caught 'em!"

Tensely they scanned the paragraphs telling of their famous father's brilliant work in capturing the men, including the head bookkeeper, who had escaped through the tunnel. At the end of the column it was stated that two of the ringleaders were still at large.

"Charlie Hinchman and Moe Gordon!" exclaimed Frank. "Maybe we'll catch one of them before long!"

A drive of several hours brought them again to High Point. Tensely they rang the bell and waited for the butler to open the front door.

"Good mawnin', gen'mun," greeted the shining-faced servant a moment later. "Mistah Webster is in his study."

The millionaire advanced toward them, his

features looking more worn and his face thinner than ever. "Good morning, boys. Please sit down," he said weakly.

"How is Narvey?" Joe asked at once.

"Narvey is no better," was the sad reply. "If anything, he is worse," Mr. Webster went on.

The Hardy boys expressed their sympathy and wanted to tell the man what they suspected, but in all fairness to Narvey they felt they should speak to the young man first. Accordingly they went upstairs alone to see him.

"Suppose he won't tell us anything," whispered Joe. "If Gordon has such a hold on him, he may be afraid to speak the truth."

"That's true," agreed Frank in a hushed tone. "I believe the best plan would be to surprise him and pretend we know more than we do."

Accordingly when they reached Narvey's bedroom, the older brother pushed open the door a little way and called in a hoarse voice, "Hello, Marko!"

"Gordon!" replied a faint voice from the bed. "Go away! Leave me alone! I haven't any more money to give you now. You said you wouldn't come back until tomorrow."

Changing their plans completely, the boys tiptoed away and returned to the first floor. There they had a long talk with Mr. Webster, relating everything they had learned at the circus. The man told them that to humor his son he had given him several large sums of cash recently.

"I couldn't imagine why he wanted the money," the man said, "but I didn't question him. He hasn't left High Point, so he couldn't have spent it."

"Narvey has been around the grounds?" asked Frank. "He hasn't remained in the house every minute?"

"My son went out a few times, always alone," the father answered. "Once when I was worried because he didn't return for half an hour, I went to look for him. But he was all right, although he seemed very excited and asked me not to follow him again."

"Probably he was giving the money to Gordon at that time," said Joe. "One thing is certain: the crook will be back, so he can be nabbed right here tomorrow."

Mr. Webster begged the boys not to leave High Point, even for an hour. His eyes were so full of fear and his tone so pleading that they agreed. They spent the balance of the day looking about the grounds, wondering where the meeting place of Narvey and Gordon might be. There were several secluded spots which might be possibilities.

"I vote for the little empty house at the edge of the estate," said Joe. "That's where I'll watch for Gordon."

Narvey appeared at suppertime and showed a forced interest in seeing the Hardy boys. He was not told they would stay all the next day; merely that they were overnight guests. He hardly spoke during the meal and immediately afterward returned to his bedroom.

"He certainly is no better," said Frank to Joe as they were undressing later. "I believe the only thing that will restore Narvey's mind is a great shock of some kind."

"Maybe," yawned Joe. "Well, good night," he added, tumbling into bed.

The village clock had just struck midnight, when there came a slight rustling sound from somewhere among the bushes directly beneath Mr. Webster's room. A shadowy figure detached itself from the shrubs and slowly climbed a stout vine leading toward an open window.

CHAPTER XXIII

THE PUZZLING ATTACK

"WHAT's that?"

Frank Hardy sat bolt upright in bed, listening intently.

"Joe, wake up! Hear that moaning?" he called to his brother.

"I don't hear anything," said Joe, yawning.

"It's time to get up anyway. It's seven o'clock," his brother told him.

Joe arose, and started to dress. He halted abruptly. "Frank! I do hear something! Listen!"

A distinct moaning sound pervaded the room. At first the boys could not decide from what direction it came. Joe went to the window and peered out.

"Nothing wrong so far as I can see, Frank."

"I think it's coming from somewhere in the house, Joe. Listen, there it goes again. It *is* a groan; there's no doubt about it."

Anxiously the boys pulled on their clothes and stole into the long corridor. The sound was distinctly louder. Again and again it came, a low, guttural groan. The boys now were thoroughly alarmed.

"Let's find the butler, Frank. Wait here, I'll get him."

Returning with the Negro a few minutes later, Joe found his brother attempting to force a locked door at the end of the hallway.

"That's Mistah Webster's room!" exclaimed the butler, his eyes rolling fearfully. "Is he sick? Lawd he'p us!"

The man was too frightened to be of much assistance to them. Joe hurried ahead to join his brother.

"Guess we'll have to break in," panted Frank. "Ready? One, two, three!"

Together the boys hurled their combined strength against the stout panel, behind which the sounds of groaning were now louder than ever. To their dismay the door failed to budge even slightly.

"It's very strongly built," muttered Frank. "We may have to get in by a window."

For a brief instant they listened to the groans, which grew more and more terrifying.

"Whatever has happened to Mr. Webster must be something pretty awful, Frank. Golly, it gives me the shivers even to listen to him."

"Me, too. Let's give this door another try."

Again and again they threw themselves against the thick wood but without success. The groaning, meantime, had all but ceased.

"Mr. Webster!" Frank called softly. "Mr. Webster, are you—all right?"

There was no answer.

"We may be too late," said Frank gravely. "Come, let's try the window."

The brothers raced downstairs and outside. "That must be his room," said Joe a few moments later, pointing overhead.

"The window's closed. That's queer. You'd think he'd have it open in warm weather."

"Maybe he shut it when he started to dress. Frank, we'll have to find a ladder somewhere."

"There's the garage. Let's have a look."

Fortunately the building was unlocked. Hastily rummaging about they did find a ladder which they quickly carried to the house. With Joe bracing its base in the soft earth, Frank climbed slowly toward the window in question. Tensely Joe watched. "See anything, Frank?"

"Not yet. I'm trying to get in."

There was a sudden grinding sound, and the window opened. Joe heard his brother gasp.

"Frank! What is it?"

"Hurry inside the house, Joe. I'll unlock the bedroom door for you."

Swiftly Frank climbed over the ledge and into the room. He unlocked the door just as Joe's footsteps sounded on the stairway. An instant later the boys were standing over the prostrate form of Mr. Webster stretched out on the floor near a window.

"He's still alive, but his pulse is very weak," whispered Frank, touching the old man's wrist gently. "Better get a doctor as quickly as possible. Ask the butler. Maybe he knows one."

The Negro was hovering in the hall not daring to look inside the room. Joe rushed up to him. "Do you know who Mr. Webster's doctor 'is?" he asked.

"Y-yes, I know, b-but I cain't think. Oh, if Mistah Webster should die an' leave that awful boy!"

Without waiting any longer, Joe dashed to the telephone in the study and called the operator.

"Send a doctor to Axel Webster's home right away," he ordered.

Putting down the receiver, he raced upstairs, where Frank already had collected some towels, soaked them in cold water, and applied them to the patient's head.

"He's sinking, I'm afraid," the boy said in a hushed tone. "He must have had a heart attack. I certainly don't see any sign of a wound on him, do you?"

Footsteps sounded on the staircase. A tall man carrying a black bag hurried into the room.

"What has happened?" he queried, looking around sharply.

Frank pointed to the millionaire's still figure, which they had laid upon the bed. The doctor began his examination. He listened to the old man's heart, and a grim expression came over his face.

"Very bad, very bad," he muttered. "The patient's condition is desperate, and I believe it's not his heart alone."

"Have you any idea what caused it, Doctor?" Frank asked in concern.

The physician shook his head. "It puzzles me. I cannot understand it. I shall administer a drug at once."

Completing the injection the doctor went downstairs to make a telephone call. In the meantime Frank had been leaning out the window.

"Joe! Come here a minute," he called in a hoarse whisper.

"What do you see?"

"Look at this vine. It's ruffled up and broken off in places. It looks as if someone had climbed it very recently. Let's go downstairs and look at it."

When the physician returned, the boys hurried below to examine the vine and the ground around it. Fresh footprints leading to the spot below the window were proof that a person with a large-size shoe had climbed to the room above on the heavy creeper.

"Maybe Mr. Webster was poisoned!" exclaimed Frank. "Let's ask the doctor."

"You don't suppose Narvey—" began Joe.

"Oh, no," said Frank quickly. "Not even under Gordon's influence. But say, it might have been Gordon himself."

"What possible reason would he have for doing such a thing?" objected Joe. "He was getting money out of the old man as it was. Why would he spoil that little game?"

Frank, thinking this over, did not reply until the boys, deciding to enter the house, reached the front door. "I wonder if Mr. Webster was going to leave his fortune to Narvey," he said. "If so, Gordon may have wanted to get a big slice of it while he still had Narvey in his power."

"You mean that if young Webster's memory should return, he'd have nothing to do with Gordon, so the crook would not benefit from the father's death?" said Joe.

"Exactly. Let's speak to the doctor about the idea of poison."

Before the boys reached the hall, a taxi pulled up to the door. Out stepped Fenton Hardy.

"Dad!" both boys exclaimed.

"What has happened here?" he asked quickly. "When your Aunt Gertrude told me you had left the circus to come to High Point, I was sure you had learned something important."

When the detective, seated in the library, had been told the whole story of what clues his sons had uncovered since he had left them, he praised them warmly. "I'm mighty proud of you both," he beamed. "Later we'll have a celebration for your good work. Right now we must continue our hunt for the missing thieves.''

''And the piece of blade marked 'Edouard,' '' added Frank. ''I want to return every bit of the weapon to Mr. Barker.''

''Don't forget that the person who sold the estoque to Castillo will have to give back the poor matador's 'one week salary,' '' chimed in Joe, grinning.

''Let's go upstairs now and see how Mr. Webster is,'' suggested his father. ''You boys tell the doctor your suspicions. It's possible the m——''

At this moment a horrible shriek resounded throughout the mansion and brought the Hardys to their feet with a bound.

''It came from upstairs,'' cried Frank, dashing from the room.

The boys ascended the staircase two steps at a time.

''Oh, oh,'' groaned a voice, and Narvey limped toward them. ''A snake bit my ankle!'' he cried, and fell to the floor.

CHAPTER XXIV

QUICKLY the boys helped Narvey to his feet and carried him into his room. He was too panic-stricken to speak for a few seconds, then he blurted out:

"It's in the hall. The terrible snake is in the hall!"

"I'll get the doctor right away," offered Frank, dashing off. "He's in your father's room."

"The doctor?" Narvey repeated the boy's words. "Why is he here?"

"Mr. Webster—your father—is very ill," replied Joe. "Didn't you know?"

The young man on the bed gave a scream of terror. "No, oh, no. This is the end!" he cried, covering his face with his hands.

Frank returned with the physician, who immediately opened his kit to take out a bottle of snake serum and administer a dose at once. As the Hardys went to the hall to look for the reptile, they saw their father in a dark corner strike at something with the legs of a chair he held in his hands.

"It's gone!" he cried as his sons rushed up. "I missed it. Be careful, boys," he warned them. "The snake may be just inside one of these doorways."

Each searcher went a different way. Frank had hardly entered one of the rooms when he stiffened. He had heard a suspicious rustling sound beneath the bed. Before investigating further he looked around for a possible weapon.

"That ought to do the trick," he muttered as his eyes fell upon a heavy cane standing in a corner. Stealthily he picked it up and leaned over, squinting into the shadows under the bed.

There was a menacing buz-z-z, followed by a slithering sound as an angry snake reared to attack him. Frank's action was automatic. Down came the cane with a terrific *whack,* followed by another, then a third.

"What's happening? Did you get it?" burst out Joe, running into the room.

He uttered a cry of relief as he saw the ugly reptile stretched out motionless on the floor. "Here it is, Dad! Frank killed it!"

Instantly his father came into the room. Joe, upon looking at the viper, exclaimed:

"That snake is exactly like the one which escaped from my circus pen!"

"Really?" said Mr. Hardy with a grave look.

"It may not be the same one, of course, but it's the same size and kind."

Frank's expression changed to one of doubt. "That's pretty farfetched, Joe. How could it have got here unless somebody carried it?"

"That's just the point, Frank. Maybe somebody *did* carry it! And that somebody was Moe Gordon! The pieces of our puzzle are nearly in place!" he exulted.

Mr. Hardy had stepped into the hall and spoken to the doctor who had just come from Narvey's room.

"If Mr. Webster's condition is due to a snake bite, his chances of recovery are excellent," the physician was saying as the boys joined them. "Now I shall be able to administer the correct treatment."

As soon as the doctor had gone, the Hardys discussed Joe's idea about Gordon.

"If your theory is right," said the detective, "and Gordon used this means to hasten Mr. Webster's end, then he is a worse criminal than I suspected. In any case, there should be a police guard here. I'll go downstairs and telephone for one at once."

The detective called the local headquarters and told the story. He asked that a couple of men be sent out disguised as outdoor workmen.

In the meantime a young man who lay on a bed in an attractively-furnished room near-by slowly arose and looked about him perplexed. As he started to walk toward a window he gazed down ruefully at his lame leg.

"How did I get here?" he asked himself. "Yes, this is my bedroom. But I ran away and joined a circus under the name of Marko. Oh yes, I remember, I fell and everything went black. How long ago was that?"

Try as he might, the young man could recall nothing from the moment he had slipped from the trapeze. "I must go and find my father at once," he decided. "I hope he has forgiven me."

The son hurried to the hall door and opened it. He was confronted by two strange boys.

"Hello, Narvey," one of them said. "Feeling better?"

"You know me?" the young man asked, smiling. "I'm sorry, but I do not recall having met you."

The Hardys—for it was they—exchanged glances. What was young Webster up to now? When they did not reply, Narvey asked pleasantly:

"Do you know where my father is?"

"Yes, we do, and you do, too," exploded Joe. "Your friend Moe Gordon fixed him up!"

"Moe Gordon?" the young man repeated. "I never heard of him."

"Now listen, Narvey Webster," cried Joe. "I don't know what you're up to, but whatever it is, it's not going to get by Frank and me!"

Frank was studying Narvey intently. Somehow young Webster seemed different. He stood up straighter, his voice was firmer, and the haunting fear was gone from his eyes. Quietly

Frank squeezed Joe's hand in a warning signal the boys sometimes used.

"Narvey, would you mind coming downstairs with us?" the older boy asked cordially. "We'd like to talk to you before you try to see your father."

"I'd be glad to," replied the other. "But—but you aren't going to tell me my Dad isn't living? Oh, I couldn't bear that! You hinted——"

"Mr. Webster is alive, but has been dangerously ill," said Frank. "However, we have every reason to believe that he will be better very soon."

The boy led the trio downstairs. Reaching the library, he quickly whispered a few words to his father who was just coming from the telephone.

"I believe Narvey's mind is normal again!" the boy said excitedly under his breath. "The shock of the snake bite plus hearing about Mr. Webster's illness must have brought back his memory."

Using this theory, Frank introduced himself, his father and Joe. He added that they were friends of Mr. Webster.

"Then I can speak freely to you," Narvey said. "I realize I must have been a victim of amnesia for some time. How long I don't know. I can recall nothing of what I have been doing since I fell from a trapeze in a circus." He smiled at his listeners. "I hope it wasn't anything I'll be ashamed of. Will you please tell me what you know?"

The three Hardys actually squirmed in their chairs. This was the hardest assignment any of them had ever been given. Yet this good-looking, affable young man before them must be told the truth, for he was the connecting link by which the law was going to catch up with Moe Gordon.

"Guess I must have done something pretty bad," said this new Narvey, as he noted the hesitancy of the boys and their father to speak. "Please don't spare me. I'd rather know."

Little by little the tale was unfolded. Many times during its recital young Webster winced, but he urged the storytellers on. At its conclusion he sat silent for several seconds, his head bowed. Then he looked at the Hardys with determination.

"I'll do everything in my power to catch this crook Moe Gordon," he said, his eyes flashing. "Tell me, how shall I start?"

CHAPTER XXV

IMPORTANT EVIDENCE

For some time Narvey Webster was coached in the part he was to play. The Hardys were not sure where the young man was supposed to meet Moe Gordon, but the little house on the edge of the grounds was chosen as the likely spot.

"There are recent footprints around it and other marks leading toward a section of fence that has been broken," explained Frank. "I believe that's the way by which Gordon comes and goes."

The probable time of meeting was guessed after Joe had consulted the butler about what hour Narvey usually left the house whenever he went outdoors. Four o'clock was decided upon and it was agreed that the boys would remain indoors so as not to be observed. Mr. Hardy, whose car still stood in front of the mansion, was to drive off at once. He would come back unobtrusively later.

Time might have hung heavily on the hands of the brothers and Narvey, had not a very pleasant interruption occurred. Just as the plans had been completed, the doctor came downstairs, a smile on his face.

"I am pleased to be able to announce that Mr. Webster is very much better," he reported. "He is completely out of danger."

"Did you find a snake bite on him?" asked Frank quickly.

"Yes, I did," the physician confirmed, "so I gave him the proper serum. He did not respond as quickly as his son, due to his age and the fact that he did not receive the antidote immediately."

"May I see him now?" Narvey asked excitedly. "I have so much to say to him."

"Yes," answered the medical man. "He regained consciousness some time ago. He is feeling weak, of course, and must stay in bed, but otherwise he is all right."

Narvey hurried from the room and went up the stairs in eager anticipation. The Hardys remained below, feeling that this reunion of father and new-found son must not be witnessed by outsiders. Later the two boys went to the elderly man's room and found the patient sitting up in bed, looking well and content.

"I am so happy I almost feel as if I could get up and dance a jig," the man said joyfully. "To think I have my son—my real son back again," he added, his eyes glistening. He then related how he had arisen early that morning to close his window and had been bitten by the snake. "Oh, I never can thank you Hardys enough for all you've done for us," he praised the boys.

"We didn't have a thing to do with Narvey's memory being restored," said Frank modestly. "In fact, it was probably the very crook who had your son in his clutches for a while who is responsible for bringing back Narvey's memory."

"You mean the shock caused by the snake bite?" Mr. Webster asked. "I see. My son tells me you have not quite finished your work and that he is to take part in a possible capture of the thief. Well, I see it is after three o'clock, so I suppose you must start." He grasped his son's hand fearfully. "Narvey, be *very, very* careful," he pleaded.

As had been prearranged, young Webster went ahead to the cottage. A little later the Hardy boys followed, picking their way carefully so as not to be observed. As they neared the cabin, they were startled by the sound of two angry voices.

"Neither of them is Narvey's!" gasped Joe. "What do you suppose has happened, Frank?"

Fearfully the brothers drew closer. Suddenly a door slammed and the conversation inside the building ceased. Standing back of the house, the boys could not see whether one person or more had left the place.

"Let's look inside," ventured Frank when they were within a few feet of an open window. "You stand guard."

Craning his neck, the boy peered inside, then drew back and returned to Joe.

"Only one person in there and he's eating cheese!" Frank muttered under his breath.

"Eating   ch—Gordon!"   whispered   his brother, his eyes blazing. "Narvey told us that Moe Gordon likes——"

"Sh," warned Frank. "I'm not sure it's he. His back was toward me."

"The person he was talking to must have left," said Joe. "We can handle one man between us. How about it?"

"All right. Wonder where Narvey is."

Stealthily the Hardys crept to the front of the little building. At a signal they burst through the doorway.

"What!" exploded a vicious voice. "Look out, or I'll——"

The boys stopped short as they found themselves confronted by a sharp, glistening blade. Gordon—for it was he—sneered at them, gesticulating with the weapon.

"Take one more step, either of you, and I'll——"

Simultaneously there was a yell from a corner of the room. To the astonishment of the boys the door of a large closet popped open and Narvey jumped out.

"I'll give you a hand!" he cried, jumping on Gordon, who struggled desperately. "Beat him up!" the young man shouted, pounding the man whom Frank and Joe now were holding tightly.

Suddenly a shadow fell across the doorway.

"Stop!" barked a voice. "Put up your hands!"

There stood Charlie Hinchman!

Joe's hand, half hidden by Narvey's body, quickly moved from his pocket to his mouth. A second later there came a shrill blast from a police whistle. Frank instantly rolled from Gordon's form and lunged toward Hinchman, who had been taken off guard by the signal.

"After him," yelled Joe as the crook whirled around to dash from the cottage.

Then came shouts outside, mingled with running footsteps. The police!

"The men have him," said a voice and Mr. Hardy stepped into the cabin a moment later. "And you have Gordon, too. Good work, boys."

In the meantime Joe had picked up the weapon the man had used. It was part of a sword blade. Quickly he looked for a name on it.

"Dad! Frank! It says 'Edouard' on here!" he cried. "Now we have all the pieces of the Crusader's sword!"

"And each piece of the broken blade was a clue to your downfall, Moe Gordon!" added Frank, looking at the thief.

The prisoner became more and more sullen as he was accused of having robbed Mr. Barker's office; of having stolen the estoque and selling it to Castillo; and of having led astray a young man whose mind was in a confused state. He denied nothing, and under Mr. Hardy's gruelling questions even admitted a few things when he learned that Narvey's memory had been restored.

"I met Marko—that's the name I knew him by—I met him one day by accident after he tried t' get rid of me," snarled Gordon. "He told me about Mr. Hardy sayin' he was a millionaire's son, so I thought I'd get some money for myself. After all, we was pals."

"But you weren't pals in trying to end Mr. Barker's life, so you could benefit from Narvey's inheritance," spoke up Frank.

"He knew about it," growled Gordon. "I told Marko I might do it. Say, I ain't goin' to take the rap for this whole thing alone," he yelled savagely.

Mr. Hardy looked at the crook with steady eyes. "Narvey Webster is no longer under your influence. And anything you made him do while he was suffering from a loss of memory cannot be held against him now."

After the police had led the man away, the others walked toward the mansion. Narvey explained that just after reaching the cottage two men had approached it, so he had thought it best to hide in the closet.

"Even when one of them left I wasn't sure he was far enough away for me to come out," he said. "For a while I was afraid our scheme wasn't going to work. Say, you don't mind if I run ahead, do you? I want to tell my father the good news."

The Hardys smiled understandingly. They too as father and sons had many things to talk over. The detective with the help of his boys had wound up successfully the mystery of the trucking thieves.

When they arrived in Bayport the boys immediately summoned Chet to the house.

"Well, we got home in time for your play," laughed Joe.

"Before we practice for it," said Frank, "we want to thank you for the valuable tip you gave us about Castillo. Really, Chet, you ought to become a detective."

"No thanks," grinned the fat boy. "Well, let me see you rehearse, then tell me about how you caught the crooks."

Hardly had the brothers started to brandish their swords than Aunt Gertrude bustled into the room. "Just what is going on here?" she demanded. "Are you two boys playing with those terrible blades again?"

"We're practicing," explained Joe. "How about coming to our show?"

The lady flushed in embarrassment. "Now, boys, you know I'm too old to go to such rough things. Anyway I'm afraid your play isn't going to be a success. You see, I know you pretty well. Probably I'd just be ready to come when up would pop your next mystery, and pff —you'd be gone!"

The boys laughed, but hoped something would pop up soon. And it was too, for more adventure was to overtake them in *The Flickering Torch* mystery.

A loud groan came from Chet. "Holy cats,

fellows, you can stay home till the play's over tonight, can't you?"

"You never can tell," said Joe with a sly wink at his brother. "Every now and then Aunt Gertrude gets a strange hunch that turns out to be exactly right!"

THE END